They had so much to do, so much to plan and learn about each other and the world they would build for their child.

They wanted the same things, even the things they couldn't have.

Jenna's brown eyes locked on his green ones.

Sebastian fascinated her.

Like magnets, they stepped toward one another, erasing the space between them in synchronized movements as if greater powers had choreographed them.

He opened his mouth.

She licked her lips.

His eyes locked on the motion, and he swallowed.

"The baby," she said.

He nodded. "We need to talk about the baby."

She nodded, heat rising to her cheeks, her skin tingling and alert. "First and foremost."

The tension between them stretched tight, egged on by the heat, and the sumptuous library, and the man she had already proved she was willing to risk everything to touch.

And then he was closing the space between them on a strangled oath, his arms coming around her.

The Queen's Guard

Romance comes to the royal palace!

When scholarly Mina Aldaba is stolen from a job interview and immediately married to the king of Cyrano, her life is totally upended. But as she adjusts to palace life, her two elite guards, Helene d'Tierrza and Jenna Moustafa, become not only her constant companions but also firm friends.

These three women will discover every inch of their strengths as they each navigate the rocky waters of romance...

Read Mina and King Zayn's story in *Stolen to Wear His Crown*

Read Helene and Drake's story in *His Stolen Innocent's Vow*

Read Jenna and Sebastian's story in *Pregnant After One Forbidden Night*

All available now!

Marcella Bell

PREGNANT AFTER ONE FORBIDDEN NIGHT

HARLEQUIN®
PRESENTS®

ISBN-13: 978-1-335-56908-0

Pregnant After One Forbidden Night

Copyright © 2021 by Marcella Bell

This edition published by arrangement with Harlequin Books S.A.

For questions and comments about the quality of this book, please contact us at CustomerService@Harlequin.com.

Harlequin Enterprises ULC
22 Adelaide St. West, 40th Floor
Toronto, Ontario M5H 4E3, Canada
www.Harlequin.com

Printed in U.S.A.

Marcella Bell is an avid reader, a burgeoning beader, and a corvid and honeybee enthusiast with more interests than hours in the day. As a late bloomer and a yogini, Marcella is drawn to stories that showcase love's incredible power to inspire transformation—whether they take place in the vast landscapes of the West or imagined palaces and exotic locales. When not writing or wrangling her multigenerational household and three dogs, she loves to hear from readers! To reach out, keep up or check in, visit marcellabell.com.

Books by Marcella Bell

Harlequin Presents

The Queen's Guard

Stolen to Wear His Crown
His Stolen Innocent's Vow

Visit the Author Profile page
at Harlequin.com for more titles.

To all the stories I've loved before.

CHAPTER ONE

FOR THE FIRST time in his life, Sebastian Redcliff gave another human being a second look.

And then he stared.

She wore the dark blue uniform of the royal guard.

Thick layers of colorful Kevlar, utility pockets, and polyester obscured the shape of her body and she wore her near-black hair in a severe and simple low braid that swung down her back. There was nothing remarkable about any of it.

Her sloe-eyed gaze was wide, like a forest doe's, and her nose straight at the bridge and rounded at the tip.

Her lips were wide, and her mouth a natural dusky rose.

In fact, if it hadn't been for her incredibly thick eyebrows, the kind that could catapult a model to international fame, there would be absolutely nothing unique or particularly remarkable about her looks.

But it wasn't her physical appearance that had led to Sebastian's uncharacteristic pause.

He was the head of intelligence for the island nation of Cyrano.

Appearances were particularly superficial to Sebastian.

But, blessed—or cursed—as he was with above average gifts in the art of seeing beneath the surface of things, he found himself ensnared upon laying eyes on her.

A blinding prism of light lay beneath *her* surface.

He had never encountered a person—man, woman or child—who exuded goodness with the intensity that she did.

Confronted with all of that earnest intention—so much delicious passion for hoping and trying, not for gain, but simply because it was the right thing to do—wrapped up in one person filled Sebastian with an imperative and irresistible urge to dive into her light.

The sky was up, gravity held the universe together and he had to quell the first thing that had ever distracted him from carrying out his duties.

His presence at the event tonight was a matter of business, an opportunity to debrief with the king while *hiding in plain sight*, as they said.

There would be no hiding, however, with a light like hers around.

Fortunately, if Sebastian had learned anything

in his life to date, it was that things tended to only look bright from far away.

Looking deeper, learning more, was all it typically took to dim the glow.

It was only the most incurable fools who remained transfixed on the item of their obsession after scratching the surface, and he was many things, but not a fool.

In all his life, he'd found nothing so effective at dimming his interest in a person as having sex with them.

Intimate knowledge, he'd found, quickly tarnished illusions.

And whatever else he knew and thought about her—which was a surprising amount given that vetting royal security records was one of his many duties—it was very certain that, paragon of dedication though she may be, she was still just a wretched human like the rest of them.

It was his job to keep that in mind, just as it was his job to remain impenetrable, inscrutable and always one step ahead.

That she'd penetrated him with her glamour, wreaking havoc on any semblance of inscrutability, was therefore an intolerance that required redress.

Right now, inscrutable was the furthest thing from what he was.

Watching her, he was filled with the feeling that if she decided to aim the high beams of all that goodness at him, he might disintegrate like a vampire in sunlight.

Or even worse, he might be flayed open and revealed with no place left to hide.

Her name was Jenna Noelle Moustafa—she was of good Cyranese stock and a dedicated member of the Priory, a small religious group, and had a record to prove it.

Sebastian had reviewed that record personally but he had never met her in person.

Officially, he still hadn't.

But he would. Within the hour, he decided then.

Jenna, as he now called her in his mind, stood watch over the Queen of Cyrano, on solo duty as her guard partner and captain, Helene d'Tierrza, was the hostess of the gala they were currently attending.

While Helene was off duty, the full complement of the king's security team supported Jenna in her role of safeguarding the queen, but even from across the balcony, it was evident that Jenna had the duty well in hand.

Her entire attention was focused on the monarch, eyeing the queen with a mixture of adoration and responsibility that went beyond what was typical of her position, almost as if she were guarding a sister.

This was apparent in not only her gaze but the way her body remained poised, ever ready to leap to defense, offense or sacrifice—whatever the situation demanded.

She did not guard her liege. She guarded her friend.

Sebastian could almost taste the dedication and commitment from across the crowded balcony.

It wasn't nearly enough.

He wanted the whole thing.

He wanted every ounce of the attention she gave the queen and more focused entirely on him.

The queen accepted dainty hors d'oeuvres from a server, and Jenna said something low to her. The queen responded with a shake of her very curly head and let out the loud, open, commoner's laugh for which she was becoming famous.

King Zayn could not have picked a better queen himself—and he had not picked her. To the king's surprise, at thirty-six years old, Zayn had learned that his father, the late King Alden, had betrothed him to a common woman, the daughter of the man who'd saved Zayn and his mother's life before he had even been born.

Queen Mina was perfect for the role—beautiful and incredibly intelligent—but more importantly for Sebastian's current purposes, she was a lovely and reliable distraction to the king.

Turning now to the king, he commented, "Queen Mina looks lovely this afternoon."

And it was true.

The queen stood out, a breath of fresh air and lively intelligence among a sea of jaded wealth. The king's violet gaze traveled in her direction before snagging on her with the hunger of a starving man.

It was clear he wanted to breathe her deep.

Sebastian almost smiled. It was all too easy.

People often made the mistake of thinking that his was the work of shadows and lies when, in fact, spy craft was and ever would be the arena of truth—who held it, who wanted it kept secret and what they might be willing to do to ensure that it remained that way.

Lies blew over, fell apart at the slightest pressure.

Truth made grown men weep and cry out for their mothers.

Truth was what snagged the monarch's attention now, made his violet eyes go dark and intense, his entire focus, at least temporarily, fixed on his much-adored wife.

"Indeed, she does, and like she needs a break. She's been in high demand this afternoon," the king added.

Sebastian smiled. To all the world, it would appear he'd shared a private joke with the monarch. But, as was often the case, all the world would have been wrong.

Sebastian kept smiling as the king made his way to his queen with his own guards alert and at a discreet distance—precisely as Sebastian had wanted. Things were going according to plan.

He loved it when things went according to plan.

He loved it almost as much as he would love the sensation of things returning to normal after he'd seduced Jenna. Once would be enough. Once was always enough.

Tasting her would disarm the intrigue and render her ordinary. Then he could forget about her.

She would cherish the memory forever because he had standards.

Afterward, he would no longer feel like he'd been scraped raw and exposed to the world, all of his shields ripped clean off by the simple fact of her existence.

He would return to being Cyrano's most notorious playboy—wrecker of marriages and despoiler of hearts.

Every spy needed a cover and with the family history he had, his mother's infidelities and wildness well known, it was only natural that his cover would be that of the heartless Casanova cad. He had become known more for being free with compliments and enjoying hedonistic delights than for his intelligence or dedication.

Covers worked best when they fulfilled people's expectations and the Redcliffs had earned a reputation thanks to the previous generation.

To the eyes of society, he was everything Jenna was not—her polar opposite.

She was a royal guard, her full heart in her duty, on proud, uniformed display. As a Priory woman, she was dedicated and faithful to her unusual upbringing and religion, as evidenced by the fact she'd made a stipulation in her employment records that she be allowed the Priory's weekly day of rest and important holidays off. The Priory were a family-focused and conservative religious minority in Cyrano, famous for still encouraging chastity before marriage in their youth and refraining from many of the modern pleasures that men like Sebastian lived and breathed.

No woman had ever cared to resist him. The sheltered, serious guard would be no exception.

And if she did turn down the pleasure he offered, well, he knew how to walk away. He was just confident she would not.

In fact, the ease with which he anticipated he'd achieve his ends only urged him to get it done sooner.

Her incessant brightness drew him like a moth to a flame, tempting him to come closer, luring him out of the shadows and threatening to both reveal and destroy the darkness he moved within.

It was his job to move in the shadows. He could not be drawn out.

The king reached the two women, and Jenna created space for him with a slightly awkward shuffle of her feet. Her frown, with those unbelievable brows coming together just so, her lips pursing, revealed that she wasn't pleased to be pushed away from her charge, even by the king himself.

Adorable.

And everything was progressing as Sebastian had designed.

After the incident with the Farden chancellor's son, it had become a joke that the queen needed no security when her husband was nearby. Like all jokes, it was funny because it was true.

Sebastian was counting on it.

Despite the libertine affectations he presented to the world, Sebastian was severe when it came to his work.

He had taken a vow to safeguard the nation and its monarchs, and no personal distractions could ever be allowed to supersede that, particularly not something as superficial and fleeting as attraction—even an unprecedented attraction.

Sebastian waited until the king leaned close to whisper in the queen's ear, watching for color to come to her cheeks as she gave a little nod, and then waited still longer for the king to lead the queen away from the party.

Then he crossed the balcony toward where Jenna stood, hoping the triumphant glint in his eyes didn't look too wolfish.

Sebastian intercepted Jenna's path into the interior of the manor as she followed the monarchs from a discrete distance. He positioned himself so that she bumped into his shoulder.

The move was obvious but had the desired effect.

"My apologies, Your Grace." Her words were automatic, delivered with a slight bow, stiff and formal, her eyes cast at the ground. She hadn't looked him in the eye, and though he'd anticipated that ingrained deference, he found himself irritated.

He wanted to see her eyes.

"Yes, well, if you'd been looking where you'd been going…" He infused his words with the aristocratic drawl that he'd been born to as much as the winning smile he'd been employing to get his way since he was a child.

Her eyes flashed up to his face.

Up to that point, things had been going according to Sebastian's plan.

Abruptly, they no longer were.

If her brightness had caused him to do a double take, her eyes froze him to the spot and tore him apart.

It would be tempting to assign their clarity,

the unflinching truth in their sable depths, to her profession, but that would be a fantasy.

Jenna's goodness was her own.

Astonishingly open and clear, her gaze demanded nothing less than complete truth. So crystalline and deep were the dark brown orbs that they tempted him to imagine that she saw things others didn't, that she could see through his layered masks, straight through to the true core of him.

But he did not give in to the temptation to believe.

She was no more aware of his multilayered existence than anyone else in their circle.

If she had been, a rose blush wouldn't have dusted her olive cheekbones, and her moistened lips wouldn't have parted.

Her stunning eyebrows came together, confusion clouding her gaze, her pupils dilating as she sucked in a quiet breath of air.

Already, his seduction was working, and if there was a level of unexpected thrill in the success, he attributed it not to the woman but to the reward of getting what he wanted.

He always excelled where he chose to put effort.

"Again, you have my apologies. I wasn't looking where I was going," she said. Her voice was sweet, as musical and genuine and unguarded as her stare.

It tasted like wildflower honey.

Lifting an eyebrow, he said, "I'll forgive you for not noticing me once. Not again, though."

His words startled her again, enough so that this time, he knew he'd caught her attention, truly caught it. Instead of brushing him off to return to her duty, she looked at him and *saw* him. Her pupils dilated, and her eyes narrowed before she said, "I'm sorry. I don't understand."

"We're in that together then."

Outright confusion creased her brow. "Excuse me?"

"I wish I could. But that would be like excusing the sun for rising and bringing all of this chaos to life. Impossible."

"What?" She had no idea what he was talking about, as his words were absurd.

Oddly, he found he couldn't help it. She made him feel strangely foolish.

Being absurd did not make him any less effective, though. "I find myself drawn to you with an intensity I cannot comprehend, Jenna Moustafa," he said.

Her expression shuttered. "Very funny," she said flatly before turning from him.

For an instant, he felt utterly adrift at her abandonment.

With his access to the strange creature he found so alluring suddenly cut off, his mind went momentarily blank, ceasing to process its various inputs as if transported to an all-white room with no windows or doors.

And then he was back on the balcony staring at Jenna, surrounded by the very wealthiest of Cyrano's very wealthy, with a strange cocktail of sensations swirling in his gut and his hand wrapped around her slender wrist.

She had started to leave, had begun to walk away from him without a backward glance.

It was no less than he would have expected from a royal guard.

She was on duty.

It wasn't her job to engage in cryptic back-and-forth with cynical aristocrats.

But when she had turned from him, a foreign thing had happened to him.

He had panicked. And in that blank instant, he had reached out for her hand.

She stared at his grip in surprise.

It was a small thing, barely the touch of a hand, but he had not meant to do it. It was— unconscious, or not—a deviation from his plan.

She met his eyes again and, as before, what-ever it was in her that needed to protect and serve shone out from them, bright and clear, with one critical difference: this time it was for him.

At that moment, she was his.

He knew it. She didn't.

"Are you okay?" she asked, searching his face.

The truth was a weapon. He knew that better than anyone else on the balcony. And though a strange, rusty, locked-away voice inside him pleaded with him to hold back, to refrain from what he was about to do, he ignored it.

"No," he said, and the word was a raw and rough syllable ripped from him. It was only the truth.

And like it always did, his weapon found its mark.

Confusion skittered across her gaze.

As suddenly as they had gone awry, his plans were back on track.

All he had to do now was tell the absolute truth, reveal how excruciatingly vulnerable he was to her, how fascinated and ensnared she had him—how helpless he was in the face of his need to be beside her. All he had to do was show her that she was in utter control of everything between them, and let himself be seen and touched.

And then he could be done with it, and no one would be the wiser.

"How can I help?"

Of course, she would ask like that, leading with goodness.

"Come with me to the library."

CHAPTER TWO

"COME WITH ME to the library."

Jenna's instincts screamed at her in warning in a voice oddly reminiscent of her mother's. The awareness of potential danger that she had honed through her training roared to life as if she stood on a catastrophic and furious battlefield rather than beside one of the most handsome men in the country on a balcony filled with pampered rich people.

Perhaps it was that those same instincts sensed a powerful undercurrent of strength in the man beside her—an undercurrent that warned her against dismissing this capital aristocrat as playing games despite the fact that his only occupation, as far as she had ever been able to discern, was seducing women.

His exploits were infamous, most so outrageous as to be unbelievable.

Encountering him in the flesh for the first time, however, coming face-to-face with his crystalline green eyes, dark heavy brow, fash-

ionably cut and carelessly swept-back bur-
nished-gold hair, and cheekbones that were so
hollowed-out that they looked like they had been
slashed into existence by a temperamental and
sensual god, she was suddenly willing to believe
that every single story was true.

Perhaps *that* was what the alarm was about—
the natural reaction of a cautious woman in the
face of a handsome playboy.

He was the kind of handsome that encour-
aged sinful thoughts and reckless behavior, but
she knew that for three very practical reasons
he posed no threat to her: she was poor, she was
plain and she was Priory.

Nearly three years into serving the palace
after completing her training at the Capital Military Academy before that, Jenna had become
very aware that those three facts disqualified
her from being considered as anything other
than service personnel. Just as her desire for
the wider world, a faster pace of life and something more than the ordinary disqualified her
from life as a good Priory woman.

Being only the second woman ever to earn
a position in the royal guard didn't help matters, either.

Unlike her partner, Helene d'Tierrza, who
was so stunningly beautiful and wealthy that
even being in uniform could not put off appre-

ciative stares, Jenna's womanhood disappeared as soon as she strapped in.

The denizens of the capital lived for the latest trends, the hottest fashions and a fast-paced lifestyle. Here, the most attractive woman in the room was the one who had mastered all of it.

That was not Jenna.

So, overriding her internal alarm systems, she nodded crisply to the handsome aristocrat.

Calculating with a private blush that the queen would be *otherwise occupied* for the next little while, Jenna determined that it would be no problem to offer her service to the duke—temporarily. Her first duty, of course, was to the queen.

But things like assisting wayward nobility improved the reputation of the royal guard, and kept her mind from the fact that if it weren't for her duties guarding the queen, she would never have believed that royals would spend so much time *otherwise occupied*.

That kind of attraction was something she expected from ordinary people, like her parents, who had six children to show for it—not from aristocrats. The lives of the rich and famous seemed driven less by warmer, homier passions and more by a relentless drive to increase their power, status and wealth.

Of course, it was different for Queen Mina who, like Jenna, was a common woman.

Perhaps that was due the credit for the earthy enjoyment so apparent in the monarchs' relationship.

Raising the wrist that the duke still held, his hand a strangely electric shackle, Jenna offered him a smile. "Certainly, Your Grace. However, you'll need to lead the way as I am not familiar with the d'Tierrza estate."

The words struck Jenna's ears like stones, accurate though they were. The d'Tierrza estate was her best friend Helene's home, and yet today was her first time visiting, and she was here not out of friendship but duty.

It was just another small reminder that while she lived and worked in this glittering world, even among those closest to her she would never truly belong.

But that was the price a Priory girl paid for venturing so far from home.

In that world, friends knew each other's homes and families and gathered together as frequently as possible.

When one was best friends with a duchess and a queen, though, both of whom were also one's supervisors, things went differently. Jenna only wished she could be satisfied with the closeness they did have, without longing for something that felt more familiar to her.

She had all the reason in the world to be satisfied with her relationships.

Jenna spent her entire days with the queen and ate dinner with Helene in the guard's common room every night, after which she retired to the quarters she shared with Helene. The three of them virtually lived in each other's pockets and continued to enjoy each other's company. That had to reflect a deeper relationship than visiting each other's houses.

Shaking herself free of this tangent, she brought her attention fully to the duke, finding it an easy thing to do with the heat of his skin a hot pulse around her wrist.

Rather than release her wrist, though, the duke briefly tightened the pressure of his fingers around her.

One corner of his mouth lifted, drawing her gaze to his sculpted lips and the carved hollows of his cheeks, where she noticed a faint hint of shadowed stubble grew.

The detail struck her. She would have expected him to be perfectly presented and clean-shaven. Like the undergirding of strength she sensed in him, the detail was at odds with his reputation.

In her experience, there were two kinds of men who allowed stubble: lazy ones and busy ones. She would have thought a man who made a profession of sexual pursuit would be neither.

Not that he didn't look good. That would be far from the truth.

And he didn't just look good. He smoldered. The longer Jenna stood in his presence, the more confident she grew that, handsome though he was, he owed his attractiveness to another thing entirely. His was the primal allure of the big bad wolf.

Thankfully, bad boys held no appeal for Jenna.

"Of course," he said, scanning the balcony as he spoke, assessing the crowd before leading them toward the interior of the manor.

And all of it without releasing her wrist.

People moved out of their way, noticing their joined hands but quickly dismissing it.

Her uniform was a form of invisibility. No eyebrows need lift at a royal guard being led away by a duke. The rigid roles and hidden layers of intrigue in the capital made the strict demands and expectations of growing up Priory seem light by comparison.

She liked to think the one had prepared her for the other. However, memorizing their route as she followed behind the duke, she reflected that nothing had prepared her for the mystery in front of her now.

What could the Duke of Redcliff possibly need from her?

She imagined she would find out soon enough as he pushed open a door that looked just like the other doors they'd passed thus far.

Like every room in the d'Tierrza mansion,

this one was enormous, but the library put all of the others to shame.

Inside, curved walls rolled like waves all around them, lined floor to gorgeously painted classical ceiling with books. A massive domed skylight drew in the seaside sun, and every nook boasted a uniquely comfortable reading area—a plush leather love seat here, a wing-backed chair next to a small table there, a cushioned and pillowed bench tucked beneath a many-paned window across the room.

The air was heavy with the hush that only tidily shelved books and blankets of fresh, undisturbed snow seemed to convey, deep and tangible, yet comforting, like a weighted blanket or a fire on a windy evening.

The library was a reader's paradise, but the Duke of Redcliff dragged them through it with a single-minded purpose that suggested he had a more specific destination in mind than just the privacy the stunning library offered.

"If I'm not mistaken, we've made it to the library," Jenna said, faintly breathless in anticipating what he might say.

What could she possibly have to offer the Duke of Redcliff?

He didn't turn to answer her, merely replied, "What I need to tell you requires more privacy than this echoey dust trap."

Jenna bristled. She might not know the floor plan, but this was still her best friend's home.

"The library is beautiful," she protested.

He didn't spare it a glance. "A library's beauty comes from its use—from the experiences and memories enveloped in its folds, the myriad worlds it contains. This library, however, is a mausoleum, built in honor of ego and enjoyed even less. Neither the current duchess nor the dowager duchess utilizes nor loves this room. Therefore, it is not beautiful but an echoey dust trap."

Casting him a sharp glance, Jenna retorted, "You seem to know an awful lot about this library for someone who doesn't live here."

At her words, he slowed and turned, mouth pressed into a firm line, expression shadowed. "I studied architecture at university. The d'Tierrza estate is one of Cyrano's most famous structures—certified Heritage. The library was built and stocked by the fourth Duke of d'Tierrza nearly seventy-five years ago. Look around."

Jenna did, the hush of the room and the quiet seriousness in his voice weaving around her like a spell. The shelves were not, as he'd accused, dusty, but upon looking more closely, she saw that the books were indeed old, most with heavy cloth and leather bindings with gilded gold lettering.

There were thousands and thousands of volumes and, scanning them, not a single modern title among them.

The duke confirmed her assessment with his next words. "There hasn't been a book added to this collection since they finished the library—a great showpiece for a grand, pointless gala much like today's. Lovely to look at, but lifeless."

It was impossible to imagine him as a student or even as a younger man. He gave the impression of having sprung into existence, fully formed as he was: leonine, feral and pitiless.

Whether or not he'd intended to reveal it, though, she now knew that buried so deeply that she couldn't even say she could see it, there was a young man who loved buildings and libraries.

"Are we nearly there? I would love to help you but will need to return to my duties soon." She tried to create distance with words while he led them around a final turn and into the most private reading nook she'd seen yet.

Hidden by bookshelves on all sides save the one they had approached from, this nook had a long, deep burgundy velvet settee centered beneath a breathtaking stained-glass window. The window's large, central motif, a dazzling kaleidoscope of vibrant reds, came together in the form of a rose exquisite enough to put Notre Dame to shame.

That this stunning window was hidden far away from the atrium, located in a place that

one would have to know about to find, under-
scored the luxury and extravagance of the whole
library.

Idly, her mind enchanted by the perfect little
spot, she wondered what other treasures this
"dead" library hid.

Leading her to the sofa, the duke guided her
to sit.

He remained standing, directly in front of
her, for a moment, just silently staring, his eyes
drinking her in, his pupils dark and dilated like
those of a hungry child standing outside a bak-
ery window.

She fidgeted under the intensity of his regard,
and then asked again, "What is it you want from
me, Your Grace?"

His emerald eyes direct and unflinching, he
said, "Everything."

He said it as if the statement was clear, ex-
plaining everything to everyone's satisfaction,
and because it didn't, not in the least, she was
irritated when she said, "What specifically?"

Infuriatingly, he said, "You," though this
time, a hint of confusion had crept into his voice.
"I need you."

Her eyebrows came together, each one so
thick and slashing that she had given up trying to tame them years ago, resigning herself
to merely plucking stray hairs here and there to
prevent a unibrow.

Suddenly, she wished she had spent more time on them.

His eyes burned with an unfamiliar heat that brought a strange fluttering sensation to her stomach.

She forced herself to stay still, refusing the urge to squirm, but the intensity of his stare set off rivulets of sparkling sensation along her skin.

"What do you mean?" she said quietly, her voice losing the earthy, steady quality she was known for in the onslaught of the man's regard.

He laughed, and the sound was as unexpected as it was entrancing.

It was creamy and musical, warm and baritone, like honey mixed with something naughty and decadent, intoxicating and dangerous like a cocktail. Or at least what she associated with the idea of a cocktail, as she kept with Priory tradition and didn't drink alcohol.

The laugh transformed him, shaved years from his jaded angles.

Sounding surprised himself, he said, "I mean I want you, Jenna, naked. Now."

For a moment, she simply stared at him, dumbfounded. His words buzzed around inside her, trying to land, trying to wash her away in sparkling sensation and pooling heat, but she was held fast by the absurdity of a man like him speaking those words to a woman like her.

And so, she began to laugh, stopping only when she realized he was just waiting for her to finish laughing and answer, absolutely earnest.

Staring up at him, laughter chased away by his gravity, she said, "You're joking."

His eyes bored into hers, his expression hovering in the land between intense desire and deep frustration. "I am not. I have never needed a woman as much as I do you."

She hadn't known until that moment how much she'd been craving words like that, how they would enter and expand inside her, warm and enveloping, grabbing hold of the stirring place deep inside her and squeezing and pulsing with a hold and rhythm she never wanted to end.

"That's absurd," she whispered, her voice losing its strength in the face of this unbelievable situation. "You don't even know me."

He shook his head. "Believe me. I am as surprised as you are."

She frowned, not liking the sound of that. "You don't make it sound like a compliment."

"It's not."

He was strained, tense, even irritated about it all—like he meant what he said about not wanting it but being powerless to do anything to stop it.

Why that did things to her, activated places that had no business activating, she had no idea.

The Casanova type didn't appeal to her. When she eventually settled down, as much as her family despaired of that ever happening, she wanted what her parents had: an enduring flame kind of love, one built entirely on mutual understanding, respect and compassion. A place to belong.

And, captivating though he was, she knew she was not going to find that with an aristocrat she'd only just met—especially one who was famous for his shocking and temporary sexual exploits.

Shoving aside the ring of truth to his words and ignoring the honesty of the attraction she saw burning in his eyes, it occurred to her with disappointment that this entire episode was likely some part of a cruel joke.

Too smart to fall for something like that, and too strong to waste any hurt feelings over it, Jenna was nevertheless frustrated with herself for not recognizing the signs earlier.

She'd witnessed plenty of playing with people's emotions, a kind of casual cruelty, amongst the glitz and glam of the upper crust.

There were some reasons she was glad she didn't truly belong in the life she lived.

Infusing stiff formality into her words, she remained seated—she didn't need to stand to be powerful—and said, "You're being completely inappropriate and, if you are lying, cruel. I am on duty and as such, you have no right to approach me with this. It is my job to protect the queen, and I am disappointed that you prioritized your pursuit of pleasure over that important task."

Her words were bold and direct and, even with all of the rule following and deference to rank and authority that she'd been imbued with at birth, still true to her nature. She might not like to rock the boat, but she wasn't weak. Whether it was her upbringing, her faith, or just because she'd lived twenty-nine years on this planet and seen the proof that lying got you nowhere repeated endlessly, Jenna believed in telling the truth. She put her whole heart into everything she did and followed her inner moral compass, no matter the pressure.

Her mother compared her to their old mule back home.

"Well said, Jenna, and I appreciate it even more as it confirms my evaluation of your character, but we both know that the queen is…*otherwise occupied*. You have the time, and you are not a coward."

That he had used the same words she'd thought privately confused her usually clear and direct perception.

He must have seen the king and queen leave the balcony, but the way he spoke hinted at more than mere observation. And what did he mean by *evaluation of her character*? Before today they had never spoken. While he lived in the capital, haunting the palace when not *otherwise occupied* himself, he had no connections to any Cyranese government branch that Jenna knew. He had no reason, nor right, to assess her.

Multiple times now, he had spoken as if he knew her, knew her mettle. How would he know if she were a coward or not?

And where did he get off dictating what she did and did not have time for?

Her temper, usually slow to rise, caught fire, as hot as the blush that scorched her skin.

He was right about one thing. She was no coward.

Coming to her feet, she said, "I don't know what kind of game you're playing right now, Redcliff, but I'm over it." Anger burned through the respect for tradition that she had, and in its void she'd imitated Helene's irreverence, dropping his title when she'd spoken to him.

Stepping closer to her, forcing her to tilt her head up to retain eye contact, he smiled before saying quietly, almost reflectively, "If you knew the kind of games I play, you'd know how ludicrous it is to suggest that I am anything but serious right now."

"I don't care if you're serious or not," she said drolly, "it's not happening." Her words were sharp and final, precisely as she'd intended, so she had no idea where the next ones came from, nor why they came out heavy, laden with an unspoken invitation. "I'm not that kind of woman."

He smiled then.

She shivered, the sensation running down her spine like the ripple of awareness through a herd when a predator neared.

He leaned forward, breaching the barrier of her personal space to bring his wicked lips close to her ear, close enough that the breath of his every word danced across her skin when he said, "I already know what kind of woman you are, Jenna Moustafa." He paused. "But what I don't know, what I long to find out, is how you taste. How you feel. How you sound when lost in pleasure."

What he said should have been outrageous.

Absurd.

But he was telling the truth.

The part of her that always knew, that was so entwined with truth itself that she could not help but know its taste and texture when she encountered it, was as certain as it was foolish to be.

She shook her head, the movement jostling the small gold hoops she wore, a gift from her mother, and marveled that such a slight sensation could rise to the surface amidst all the turbulent sensations warring inside her. "That's… crazy…" Her words were light, airy, the breathless, flimsy things that a different kind of person might utter.

He nodded, still so close that she could feel the heat of his skin on hers. "Utterly insane and true nonetheless. No woman has ever had this effect on me."

"You've slept with hundreds of women…" The words should have been enough to dampen the heat of the moment. Nobody liked to have their past thrown in their face, but he only smiled, the absolute lack of shame in his gaze an aphrodisiac in itself.

"All the better to please you with, my dear Jenna."

Breath escaped her, fled her parted lips like a caged bird who'd noticed the door had been left unlatched.

"I—" she started. His lips brushed against the point where her jaw met her neck, butterfly light, and her eyelids fluttered closed.

"You are singular, in the entire world, Jenna. This has already gone beyond a mere seduction."

Desperate to escape the spell he was spinning, she grasped at straws. "I can't. I've never—" And yet, she realized with astonished horror, her body coming alive in ways she'd never known possible, she *could*.

"I know," he said, the look on his face hungry and dark.

In the face of all that power and gravity centered on her, she realized she could all too easily.

He didn't just want her. *Want* was too weak a word for the fire that burned in his eyes.

The pull of it was overwhelming. She wished she could claim the magnetism between them stemmed completely from outside herself, that his need for her, how it poured off him, was responsible for the force of *her* attraction to *him*, but she could not. It would have been a shameful lie to blame what was building and blossoming entirely on him—though his words flowed over her like silk—when she knew that at least half of it erupted from within her, a seed of desire heretofore unknown bursting to life.

Who was this man, this creature of pleasure and luxury—a man she had only ever seen in passing and the exact kind of man to whom she had been invisible over these past three years—who seemed so driven to have her?

And why did the fact of it make her body smolder and heat?

Like glass in a kiln, the reasons, even the need for reasons, could not withstand the growing fire between them.

There was nothing gentle in her resistance melting away, just like there was nothing gentle about the way he was seducing her. Everything between them was up front and direct about its own dangerousness. Just like the man himself.

As if a dam had burst within her, twenty-nine years of chastity exploded at him, rushed at him in a wave so powerful that he was no longer the one driving the momentum of their seduction, but her.

Her fingers came to his hair at the exact moment his hand cupped the back of her skull and tilted her face upward.

She caught the flash of fierce green fire in his eyes before he descended, devouring her in a kiss that was more like a conflagration.

Her skin ignited everywhere on contact, exuding heat and glow so intensely that she knew that despite the circumstances, despite everything that was so very wrong with this, this moment and this man were exactly right—the union for which she had kept faith all these years.

And even still, there was no time for any of it. They had already wasted too much time talking. All too soon she would need to return to her duty.

Urgency drove her fingers, as confident and persistent in removing buckles and releasing the latches of her gear in front of him as they were in writing reports and disarming sparring opponents.

Her inner voice had spoken and she wasted no time with trepidation.

Like with the bawdy pre-wedding rituals that Priory folk guffawed through, her faith taught that there was nothing wrong in physical love, no practice taboo, so long as both parties entered into it with their hearts joined and open, willing and eager to find joy in each other's bodies.

Her faith also taught that physical intimacy was a sacred bond between paired souls, each made to soothe and comfort the other. She accepted that, took it as fact, but she had never anticipated that she would recognize her pairing at first meeting—let alone feel it with such certainty. Nor had she ever imagined that she would feel her partner's hunger for her as a tangible thing.

But she did. Awareness and, of all things, understanding of him thrummed through her body and bones and even teeth. Hot, electric, almost magical—in no way like the practical fantasies of a woman whose greatest romantic hope up to this point had been to end up with someone she found both attractive and kind.

Instead, her destiny stood before her—gorgeous, dangerous, and as far from kind and tame as it was possible to be.

He was nothing like she had imagined, yet he was hers, matched her in a way that she didn't understand and had never experienced before—neither in the world of the capital nor her Priory community.

And they had already delayed this moment for too long. Not merely over the afternoon, but throughout their lives up to this point.

CHAPTER THREE

SEBASTIAN HAD SEEN more naked women than he could count or remember.

Jenna erased any recollections that remained.

Her body was a work of art.

Her efficiency, her matter-of-fact lack of artistry in removing the layers of her uniform, should have been off-putting to a man who had been entertained by the world's most accomplished sex kittens.

It wasn't.

Instead, the deft and direct work of her fingers was the most erotic dance he'd ever witnessed.

Fully revealed, she was swarthy, her freckled skin olive, the soft hair on her arms, legs, neck dark, and at the V of her thighs thick and glossy.

Like her eyebrows, the liberal hair on her body simply accentuated rather than detracted from the perfect and straightforward beauty of her form. It drew the eye to the slender length of her forearm, the elegant arch at the nape of her neck, the shadowed and graceful contours of her shoulder blades, a natural accent and frame to her raw beauty.

As feminine as it was, her body was also extremely fit—toned and defined, as he would have expected of any person who had made a profession out of using their body as a weapon.

Her breasts, on the other hand, defied her chosen life, full and round, each one more than a handful and proud of it. Those breasts spoke of happy families and sunny hillsides—images that generally repelled him but somehow now only enhanced the fantasy of the moment.

Unsurprisingly, her bra was simple and white.

However, whilst he would have expected plain cotton, the garment was made of lace and paired with a matching pair of lace panties. Unusually, thick and durable, the material he was so familiar with seeing on women looked new on her and he suspected it was handmade.

What a security guard was doing wearing a small fortune's worth of handmade lace undergarments, he had no idea, but the effect was breathtaking.

In her ability to arrest him, to stir him past control merely by seeing her—she was truly as singular as he'd claimed.

Nothing he'd said to her thus far had been a lie.

He was, however, beginning to wonder if one taste would have the quelling effect he anticipated. Putting to rest the mystery of what lay beneath the stiff blue of her uniform certainly hadn't.

It had only stoked the fire.

When she moved to take off her bra, he stopped her with a fingertip to her plump lips. Her eyes fluttered to his, and he felt the earth shift, filling him with an urgent need to hold on as everything changed around him, though the only sound in their secluded library alcove was their weighted breathing.

Having undressed faster than her, he stood nude, entirely at ease in his form. A lover had once teased him that it was easy to be comfortable when one was built like he was, but his ease went deeper than that.

He was comfortable in the nude because it was possible to learn so much about people when one was naked. *What they liked…* Jenna's eyes lingered over his chest and shoulders, trailing across his skin like the brush of a feather. *What they were ashamed of…* Her cheeks flushed as her gaze traveled down his chest, slowly, painstakingly if he were being honest, before lighting on the appendage that stood out proudly at the apex of his thighs. *What they were afraid of…* Her breath stopped, her pupils dilated and froze, eyes remaining locked on his sex organ for an eternity before she finally gave a small gasp and her eyes darted back up to his face.

Again, her stare captured him, in a way only hers seemed to have the power to. This wouldn't stop, not until he had experienced the profound uniqueness of encountering her.

Why did her eyes freeze him in time and space?

They were an unflinching walnut color, each iris lined in kohl as if an Egyptian queen had designed their depths.

Shielding the enormous almond-shaped windows of her soul were eyelashes so densely packed it looked like she wore mascara when, in truth, she wore no makeup at all.

Everything about her was fresh and honest— her entire self, out on display for the world to see.

For him to see at the moment.

"Take out your braid." His voice was a rasping command, harsh and more desperately revealing than he would have liked.

She shook her head. "You do it." Her voice was thick but smooth; sweetness turned into nourishment like honey.

Though he noted the defiance, he chose to comply, turning the act of reaching slowly behind her to grasp the end of her long braid and draw it to him, over her shoulder, cool and soft between his fingers, into a seduction.

She was breathless before he began to release the braid.

When he loosened the last of its weave and

brought his fingertips to her scalp to massage and shake her glorious mane free, she moaned.

The sound was a molten rod down the center of him, threatening to melt and combust at the same time, but his fingers kept their rhythm and she leaned in closer, her pebbled nipples grazing the fine blond hairs on his bare chest.

He couldn't have her all the ways he wanted to, not like this, not in the library on her ever-shortening break, and the thought infuriated him. Made him want to steal her away for as long as it took to exorcise this strange demon she'd freed.

Her hair was magnificent. Long, flowing down to her waist at its longest point, it was so dark brown it was nearly black and shined like an heirloom sable. There was a wave to it, and standing there before him, her hair flowing around her, breasts free, nude but for her white lace panties, framed on both sides by the enormous stained-glass rose, he knew how man had felt upon his first sight of woman.

And at that moment, he realized he would be willing to follow *this* woman out of paradise and into the very depths of hell if she wanted him to.

She had the power of a destroyer.

It was his duty to worship her.

Dropping to his knees in front of her, he pulled the panties down over her hips and began to pray.

She tasted like peaches and fresh cream, slick, sweet and addictive.

In answering the question of how she tasted, instead of satisfaction, he only found the knowledge that hers was a flavor he wanted more of. Perhaps an endless supply.

On either side of him, her knees buckled, and he steadied her, his long, strong fingers digging into her firm thighs to the chorus of her stifled gasps and moans, her fist clenched in her mouth to muffle the noise she couldn't quell.

In no time at all, she was cresting, tipping, falling into the abyss, her body desperate to melt, her legs full of electric jitters, her breathing ragged, even around her fist. But she remained upright, steadfast even in the face of the most pleasurable death.

His grin was wide. He would bring her to her knees.

But first, he would lift her up.

Coming to his feet, he tugged her left leg up his side, enjoying the silk caress of her thigh sliding along his body. He lifted her other leg quickly, carrying her weight easily, impatient now that he'd tasted her.

He wouldn't have her standing, though.

He carried her to the scarlet settee and laid her down, captivated by her utter refusal to look away.

Eye to eye, she let him see her every response.

Such openness, such intense vulnerability, made his skin feel stretched and tight.

Without words, her eyes told him that she trusted him.

A raw, rejected thing in him snarled in the face of that trust, was tempted to warn her away, even as he laid her back with the utmost care. That was the kind of naivete that got one in trouble.

She believed in him. She accepted the unfamiliar and overwhelming energy that flared between them every time his skin made contact with hers, trusted it to keep her safe.

He, at least, now knew enough to recognize the energy for what it was—folly.

He had been wrong about seducing her.

He realized it as his hand fisted in her hair, releasing its aroma as if he'd crushed the petals of a bouquet instead of angled her chin upward to feast on her neck, covering her with his kiss.

They were where they were, and there was no going back, but he should never have tried to taste her. He realized that now.

He should have excused himself from the king's presence and left the gala immediately.

Like with every great tragedy, hubris had led him to this downfall. Rather than sating his curiosity, his sample of her had him addicted.

But it was too late to turn back now.

Too late, as his hand trailed down her neck

and chest, stopping only to cradle and adore the full globe of her breast before continuing on its silken exploration, destined for the sensitive bud at the top of her center.

She moaned when his fingers found their goal, his gentle circular caresses a blend of soothing and pressure that acted like a bellows on the still-glowing embers of her pleasure.

As he'd intended, her body tensed as the intensity built once again.

He brought her to the precipice once more with his hand, watching her face, her eyes having shut tight in pleasure, with the sharp focus of a raptor as he held her, teetering, on the edge. With his other hand, he maneuvered the condom he'd left discretely by the settee, hidden in the folds of his earlier discarded clothing. Other lovers had been impressed by the dexterity with which he could unpackage and apply the contraceptive one-handed, but the skill was more for his cover as a playboy than any desire to impress.

Rising over her while keeping her balanced on a delicious razor's edge, he repositioned their bodies before leaning down near her ear once more.

"Sweet Jenna," he murmured.

She moaned, the sound as sweet as the name he'd called her.

"Jenna, I'm going to have you now."

He felt the rush of heat, the flush of her skin, the catch in her breath at his words. She was trembling beneath him, and it was still not enough.

Her strong legs hooked around his waist, instinct urging her to close the space between them, but he still held back, retaining what was left of his fraying control.

With one hand, he played her like an instrument. With the other, he positioned himself at her entrance, rubbing along the molten crease at her center.

It was a torture, of sorts, but one he relished.

This was a singular moment between the two of them. He knew once would never be enough, but never again would he have her for the first time.

He was helpless in the face of her so he made them both suffer—edging until her lips wept for release, above and below.

Taking her in, her skin flushed and taut, her dark nipples erect peaks at the top of her full breasts, he growled, "I'm going to have you now, Jenna. You're all mine."

Once again, she cried out, her body tensing, her arms grasping and holding on to him for an instant before her hips found the rhythm.

Then they were dancing, her body's eager athleticism and soul's open brightness combining to make her a natural lover.

As natural as the fit of her—hot and slick and gripping him as he slid in and out.

Losing himself to the sensation, he only gradually became aware of the fact that his mind played a single word on a loop in rhythm with each thrust: *mine.*

He struggled to reject the idea. He was aware enough to know that something dangerous lurked in the shadows of this desire, even if his body was too busy staking a claim to heed his mind's warning.

He had made a mistake in tasting her once. It would be an easy thing to not do it again.

She was *not* his.

His mind disagreed.

His body disagreed.

The shriveled and dry thing in his chest disagreed.

With a final desperate thrust, he seized control, wrestling it back from the demon that hunted him. He was intent on denying these possessive feelings.

He was the spider in the nest. He was the shadow man pulling the strings.

He was not the one ensnared.

But when he opened, casting himself over the precipice, his mouth and soul in unison cried, "Mine."

And because she was his, she came, too.

CHAPTER FOUR

THE EMERGENCY ALARM system went off at the end of Jenna's long, contented sigh, robbing both of them of the liquid ease that seemed to have melted their bodies together on the sofa.

Separating and leaping to their feet in one motion created an awkward space between them that, for Jenna, the heat and contentment she had been filled with rapidly drained, was replaced with a sense of unease, like soapy water spilling over the edge of a mop bucket.

The alarm pattern did not signal the type of emergency she needed to rush away to deal with, but it certainly brought home a few sobering realities.

Royal emergency or not, it was her duty to be beside the queen when an alarm went off, which she was decidedly not.

And the reason for that was because she had just made love for the first time in her life in her best friend's library.

With a stranger.

No longer caught in the spell of his regard, aware only of the tingling wreckage of her own rapidly chilling passions—the emergency system sounding around them—the truth of that was becoming harder to ignore.

She didn't know this man at all and yet now she *knew* him. Biblically.

But that's not true at all, her suddenly wonky inner compass argued. *Your body recognized him as The One.*

I literally met him today, she argued with herself, unwilling to allow any excuses as she rapidly dressed. If anything, her body had merely recognized him as sexy.

She had been irresponsible at the very least, because as she continued to dress, she was most importantly not where she was supposed to be when an emergency alarm sounded. She should be at the queen's side.

She had no idea where the queen even was.

But you found him, a dreamy inner voice sighed.

The sweet, girlish part of her didn't seem to care that she'd neglected her duty and compromised her morals.

Because you haven't, it insisted. *He's The One.*

Her voice of reason gave a mental snort.

She didn't believe in that nonsense.

Not believing it was just one of the myriad reasons why she had eschewed Priory tradition—and the advice of both her parents and her older brothers—and gone to the military academy rather than straight into marriage.

She had tried to tell them that while she didn't see anything wrong with their choices, for herself she wanted a full life and career—opportunities to meet people with common interests and values—rather than chasing after notions of soul mates and rushing headfirst into motherhood.

They had called her foolish and insisted that the right life partner was the key to finding those things. They'd agreed to disagree and shaken their heads even as they sent her off with care packages.

But she hadn't minded. She'd been sure she would prove them wrong.

Back then, before she'd spent years living as an equally unrealized human being for the opposite reasons, she had been confident in her sense of the path—prideful even.

She had thought of herself as above the limiting conditioning of her childhood.

If the last few years and whatever had just happened between her and the duke were any indication, however, she shouldn't have been so sure.

Clearly some of that childhood conditioning had taken root, lying in wait to strike, ready to jump at the first opportunity to blossom and bloom in her psyche.

Was it any wonder she had given herself away to a virtual stranger then? Was it any different from all the other Priory girls she'd grown up with?

And did it even matter now that she'd gone wrong from both ends?

She'd eschewed and scoffed at finding The One, and then jumped into bed with the first man to notice her since she left her hometown.

And there hadn't even been a bed.

No matter how different life was in the capital, there was no equation in which she could make her behavior with the duke square with that of the woman she had always been.

He's not a stranger.

The persistently hopeful voice inside her was getting irritated.

He is an absolute and literal stranger.

The practical voice could get irritated, too.

But instead of offering a fiery retort, her voice of hope gave up, flipping her stomach over in the process. She suddenly felt sick, ashamed and overwhelmed.

Both voices spoke in unison now.

What were you thinking?

But she would sort the answer to that question out later, when she had some time and was alone.

Right now, she needed to get back to the queen.

She should have never come to the library with the duke.

His devilish green eyes, his mesmerizing words, his thrilling touch, his magnetic desire—all of it was none of her business.

Her business was the queen.

"Jenna!" His exasperated tone brought her attention back to the real, flesh-and-blood man, as opposed to the mental image she could neither rectify nor justify.

"What?" Her tone was short, snapping, the one she used on family when they irritated her, not on the Cyranese nobility it was often her job to protect and serve.

"The alarm. It's not for the queen."

"What?" she repeated with the same crossness.

"The queen is not in danger."

"What? Yes, I know." She frowned, his words finally penetrating her growing fog of self-recrimination. "Why do *you* know, though?" she asked. He didn't, as far as she was aware of, have any kind of background in security or defense to interpret the alarm.

"It was not a royal defense code."

She paused her furious movements, reassembling the layers of royal blue to at least look like a guard even if she couldn't seem to behave like one.

He was right. But why did he know that?

The oddity of his insider's knowledge only emphasized the *off*-ness of everything she'd done with him.

Her awareness of the enormity of it was only growing.

Something was wrong with her mind. It had to be, for one person to have knocked her so far awry from her usual way of being.

Looking around their sensual alcove, she had no justification for how she'd come here.

In the streaming light and hush of the library, hindsight made it clear what the kryptonite had been.

A savior complex, a lifetime of baseless fairy tales, and the practiced seduction of a consummate professional.

She'd been an absolute fool.

He was *not* the one. He was the Duke of Redcliff.

Frowning, she worked her way through the buttons of her shirt.

His long hands—the wicked hands that had forever changed her—came to her shoulders, pulling them forward just slightly to angle her face up.

His expression was as shuttered now as it had been clear and readable to her earlier—handsome, yes, but inscrutable, like the moon.

She didn't know anything about this man she had shared herself with.

But it was too late to take it back now.

"I'll take you back to the balcony. With the alarm, the king's guard will have ensconced her. No one ever needs to know."

His words were barbs, even if they were practical. He spoke not of the turmoil in her heart and mind—or *his*—but of the matters at hand.

She opened her mouth to say as much, but no sound came out.

His expression cracked, pain and need once again raw on his face, and he too seemed on the verge of saying something, only to be cut off by the sound of rapid footsteps approaching.

Quickly, he thrust her behind him, blocking her, if only partially, from the person coming for them directly.

"I thought I'd find you here, Sebastian. It's Hel, she's gone—" King Zayn's voice, crisp and concerned, had preceded him, but when he came around the corner, his hands occupied with buttoning the final two buttons of his own shirt, he saw the two of them, Jenna's blue uniform unmistakable, and stopped.

Famous violet eyes darted between the two of them, taking in their state of undress.

Weariness and disappointment darkened his expression.

"So, this is where you were," he said, the words clearly directed at Jenna. He sounded tired, his voice so filled with disappointment that Jenna's heart cracked.

"Your Majesty—" she began, but the king stopped her with a palm.

"We looked for you before I left the queen with my guard. She wanted to know you were safe."

Jenna's heart turned to stone in her chest. "Your Majesty, I—" she repeated.

He shook his head, shoulders burdened by what she saw was coming.

The weight came, she knew, not because he respected Jenna as a professional, though he had already shown he did by appointing her to the queen's guard in the first place, but because he knew that what he was about to do would hurt his wife. Until this moment, it had been Jenna's privilege to come to know how deep their unspoken bond was.

The crack in Jenna's heart fissured.

The king was the king, light-years away from those tasked with guarding him.

She had known, respected and protected him for the bulk of her career but felt no closer to him than the sun.

But the queen…the queen was her friend.

Jenna's throat thickened with tears, but she straightened her spine, coming to full attention for what she knew would be her final address from the king.

"You know it pains me to do this, Moustafa…"

"Zayn," the duke spoke up, the king's given name as casual on his lips as it was on Helene's. Every time it was uttered, it was a small reminder that while she had a role in the room, she wasn't like the others.

With a word, he cautioned against the king's haste, but Jenna shook her head, the gesture firm and serious. What had happened between the two of them in the alcove was between them, just as what transpired now was between her and the monarch.

And though she dreaded what was coming, she knew the king was right. Regardless of the fact that it seemed that the duke had greater access to it than most, Jenna refused to give him all of her integrity by letting him try to save her from the consequences of her actions.

"It has been an honor to serve Queen Mina. Please tell her that." Jenna's voice caught on *please*, but she would not hold the request back. Mina had to know. "And Hel—"

Her friend's name brought the monarch's attention back to the business that had him seeking out the Duke of Redcliff in the first place. "That's right. Someone kidnapped Helene."

The words were a blow to the gut.

Someone had kidnapped Helene? She would not have thought that possible. Helene d'Tierrza was not a woman who was easily taken.

But then again, Jenna hadn't been, either.

"Zayn, you can't really fire her. You were busy. If I'm not mistaken, her contract stipulates that your guard staff is sufficient in such instances—"

Surprised, the king's natural abruptness escaped in his reply to the duke. "There are more pressing matters at hand. We're meeting in my office to strategize a plan. Be there as quickly as you can be."

If it was odd that the playboy duke knew about her contract stipulations and was being invited to a war council on what to do to rescue her partner and best friend, it was nothing compared to the devastation that the king was not inviting her.

With a final sad glance her way, the king did a rare thing and repeated himself. "We looked for you." And then he turned and left, and it was once again just Jenna and the duke in the not-so-private library alcove.

"Jenna, I—" the duke started. She forestalled him with her own raised palm.

Sebastian, she thought, recalling the name the king had used. The Duke of Redcliff's first name was Sebastian.

Shaking her head, she said, her voice thick with the knot in her throat from her whole world falling apart, "Helene."

The name was all she could get past that knot, and even that came out as a croak.

His emerald eyes locking on hers one final time, he nodded, his Adam's apple moving as he swallowed whatever it was he wanted to say.

She didn't want to hear it. Whatever it was, it wasn't as crucial as Helene.

He had asked her to come to the library. The least he could do was help save her friend, whatever strange role there was in that for a Casanova.

And she would go home. There was nowhere else to go. In the dusty old library, she had burned her life to ashes.

Nothing would ever be the same.

Stepping close one last time, he kissed her on the forehead between her eyebrows. The impression of his lips branded her as surely as any scarlet letter. There was no apology in the motion.

Watching him go, the bits of everything she'd built ashes in his wake, she pondered the reality that she—steadfast, trustworthy, dependable, never-make-a-fuss Jenna—had proven every cautious mother of the world right today.

She had torched her reputation, lost her calling and home, and lost both of her best friends—one literally—in one fell swoop.

Nothing in her life would ever be the same, and it wasn't even five o'clock.

CHAPTER FIVE

IT HAD BEEN forty days since he been with Jenna in the library.

In just forty days, his entire world had collapsed.

Sebastian stared at the report on his screen without seeing it.

Blood roared in his ears, but the only sign of his agitation was the single finger rapping on the gleaming hardwood of his desk.

Jenna was carrying his child.

He was going to be a father.

Pinching the place between his eyebrows with the other hand, he released a long sigh and pushed his chair away from the desk.

He was going to be a father.

The reality of it, here and now as opposed to an unmoored and vague concept happening *somewhere in the future*, was nothing like he had imagined it would be, and, as usual when things weren't going according to his plans, Jenna was at the root.

He would never marry—not after a childhood spent as the collateral damage of the sloppy and public disaster that his parents' marriage had been—but he had always anticipated fathering children.

Continuing the family line was the only thing he truly owed his ancestors in exchange for his life of incredible wealth and privilege.

The next head of the Redcliff clan, however, had been going to be born of a surrogate, chosen with the utmost care by himself, a man with access to all the information in the country.

He would then raise his child himself, keeping said child at his side because that made the most sense, and was the safest option for the offspring of a man in his line of work and in his wealth and status bracket.

His decision had nothing to do with being thrust away from his own home at such a young age—never to be with his parents at home again—nor did his decision have anything to do with the circumstances under which he had been sent away.

He had simply spent enough time revisiting the mistakes of his parents and past to ensure that he avoided their pitfalls and failings entirely. Love and marriage had destroyed his parents, and in particular his father. The emotion and the institution had constricted both of them, squeezing every last drop of decency out until all they had left to give their child was resentment, guilt and spite.

Sebastian's child would fare better.

His choices were simply a matter of practicality.

But then there was Jenna.

Jenna was everything he would have chosen in a surrogate and more—beautiful, exceptionally healthy, fit and strong, highly intelligent, determined, diligent, steady, compassionate, honest…the list went on, and on, and on, and on.

In fact, it was the endless list of on and on that was the problem.

Jenna was *too* ideal, too much of everything he wanted crammed into one woman.

He'd spent enough time brooding about it since leaving her in the library to know for certain.

In fact, the only way he'd been able to focus up to this point had been to review her intelligence file daily, noting every small new detail as to where she was and what she was doing. As former royal security, it was procedure to monitor her whereabouts and activities for the first two years post-employment. That review just didn't typically fall to the director of intelligence.

Outrageous though his behavior had been, the instinct had been sound. How else would he have learned about his child? From Jenna?

Would she have come to him on her own?

Given what he knew of her, he trusted so.

But how long would it have taken her?

She hadn't taken or returned any of the calls she'd received from the palace, nor from her now returned former partner in the queen's guard, the newly minted Duchess Helene Andros, very recently d'Tierrza—that family name was now defunct.

If Jenna was not speaking with those closest to her, how long would it have taken her to tell him she was carrying his child?

Whatever the answer, it didn't matter now. He knew, and therefore he was compelled to act.

If it was his job to know things, it was also his job to pivot in the face of new information.

He was going to be a father.

Though most would never have believed it, he liked children. They were honest and, in some ways, more skillful at manipulating the people around them than his most talented operatives. Obviously, *his* child would be even more so.

The corners of his mouth quirked up at the idea, followed by a flashflood of images of what a child of his and Jenna's might look like.

They would have their mother's eyes, he decided.

Fathomless brown eyes, a brilliant mind, and if they happened to exude the same glow of goodness as their mother, he would simply protect it with all of the vast resources he had at his disposal.

He had planned on a surrogate because he would never subject himself or his child to the humiliations of love and marriage—that part of his plan would remain intact. So, while he hadn't anticipated Jenna's presence, nor the timing, she had not entirely upset his plans. In fact, she'd enhanced them. Now his child would have a mother as well, and in that, they could do no better than Jenna.

He did not even need to be around examples of good mothering to know, and he never really had been.

After his experiences with his own mother, he had avoided seducing or even associating with mothers. The idea of being the kind of man his mother brought home—the ones who weren't his father, as well as his father himself—filled him with disgust.

While he knew many wonderful mothers socially, their love and care for their children very evident in their behavior, they didn't move in the kind of circles he did. The ones in those circles were like his own.

The danger in Jenna being the mother of his child was not an issue of her character, however. It was in her appeal to him. In the way he hadn't ceased craving her, his desire only growing in her absence.

The danger with Jenna as the mother of his child was that he might disappear into her as his father had his mother.

His parents had fallen into each other like dolphins into a fishing net, a deadly entanglement that had ended in a wreck at the bottom of the sea and left no room for anything—or anyone—else.

And while the sea might be a metaphor, his mother *had* died in a wreck. A nasty one involving a motorcycle and winding cliff-side roads, strong intoxicants and a much younger man.

Not the cliffs of Redcliff, though. That was where her then thirteen-year-old son had been in residence, alone for his spring break.

She and her lover had died in Greece.

His father had called him from the capital to tell him, drunk and weeping.

In a way, it was true too, to say that his father had drowned. It had happened slowly and in alcohol, but it had been a drowning nonetheless.

Sebastian might not know exactly how to parent, but his parents had given him a stunningly good example of what not to do.

And, if he was lacking in the basic necessary traits that inspired a parent's love, he was at least *deeply* effective at existing. He collected and digested information like no other, was a virtuoso in effectively disseminating its nutrients to their highest and best use with a speed and efficiency unmatched.

Just not when it came to Jenna.

When it came to Jenna, his plans had the strange habit of backfiring wildly.

It wasn't an understatement to say that she had entirely upended his life—more so, in fact, than he had already been willing to acknowledge. And that was considerably, as he could admit to himself that he hadn't been right in the head since the moment he'd laid eyes on her at the gala.

He had intended to rid himself of an intoxicating mystery.

If she had been like any other woman, he would have lost interest in her and moved on.

It had been a logical, if mistaken, course of action.

He had wanted to return her to invisibility, so that she was just another body in blue he barely saw. He had not intended to make her disappear from her own life. He had certainly never intended for her to become a permanent fixture in his.

He'd used protection, for heaven's sake.

But, as he was slowly beginning to understand, where Jenna was concerned, his plans and intentions didn't matter.

Of course, their encounter would constitute a statistical anomaly.

It hadn't been enough that she'd already intruded on his mind constantly.

How could he be expected to function at all, now that he knew she was going to have his baby?

As a future duke or duchess, his child would be vulnerable. As the child of the head of Central Intelligence, even more so.

To his own mind, Sebastian was first and foremost an intelligence professional. However, it was an inescapable reality that he was also a Redcliff—*the* Redcliff. Regardless of the circumstances of their conception, any child of his would become a duke or duchess after him and would require all the appropriate protection. Managing that and keeping tabs on Jenna, both at a distance, while running his espionage empire would be impossible.

Therefore, he wouldn't do it.

CHAPTER SIX

SHE WAS PREGNANT.

After dragging her feet and then overcompensating by using more at-home tests than was recommended, Jenna had still refused to accept the positive results, but was now faced with the family doctor's prognosis, which now replayed in her mind on a continuous loop—relentless and undeniable.

Jenna was pregnant. She was going to have a baby, and not just any baby, but the Duke of Redcliff's baby.

She was intimately familiar with how it had happened, but it was still unbelievable.

And to think, she'd been under the impression that the worst had already happened, that losing everything she'd worked and built toward her whole life was the bottom of the pit.

Here was proof to the maxim then, that things could *always* get worse. She'd been caught in flagrante delicto with a man she'd just met by a man whom she had sworn to protect—a man who she respected and whose respect in return had mattered to her—and that was all in addition to losing the career she had worked for her entire life.

But if there was an oldest crime in the book, then there was also an oldest consequence, and what had befallen her thus far wasn't it.

Babies were.

Happy, chubby babies who thundered into the world and left nothing the same in their wake. Babies who deserved the entire world and the best start.

And all Jenna had to give hers was a disgraced single mother.

As to what their father would be willing to give, she realized, nauseous and dizzy at the same time, she had no idea... She didn't even know his phone number. Had no idea how she would get in touch with him to let him know.

How would he react? Numbly, it occurred to her that he might deny it. What if he forced her to prove it? Or worse, what if he asked her to end it?

Her hands came to her belly protectively. She might not have planned for it, but she would not lay down the responsibility now. She had transgressed her code of conduct, but she had not completely given up the values she had been taught. While the Priory taught that individuals had God's blessing in the governance of their bodies, they also taught that children were gifts from God.

She had apparently been chosen to receive such a responsibility-laden gift as a result of proving just how far into the depths of irresponsibility she had been willing to travel.

How easy it had been to go too far with Sebastian.

Making a disgusted noise, she tried to shake the thought of Sebastian out of her mind, scrub away the lingering want of him, to snuff out the terrible candle burning inside her, a flame at both ends—one, the ever-present desire to taste him again, the other shame.

Shame that her recklessness meant that the father of her child was a virtual stranger to her—regardless of how magnetically attracted to him she had been at the time. Shame that she had been so caught up in him that she'd not even considered the possible outcomes, but most of all, shame that in the face of the most transformational news she had ever received, the one feeling she could not seem to muster was joy.

CHAPTER SEVEN

THE TEMPTATION TO watch her sleep existed but Sebastian resisted the urge. He'd come to talk, not to gawk.

She *was* beautiful, though, in her lilac-colored nightgown.

That she wore a nightgown surprised him. Almost as much as his reaction to the bare foot and calf that peeked out from beneath her quilt. The intimacy of her bare foot struck him with more power than he'd have thought possible. He'd seen it before in the library, but had barely noticed. There had been no time to savor the full feast of her then. Now, as the only bare skin he could really see, he could appreciate that her foot was shaped like an artist's model's, defined with a high arch. The more he observed her up close and personal, the more he saw of her subtle hidden beauties—hidden not because they were hard to find but because they were so far from the first thing you noticed about her. It came as a surprise to realize that a woman who was so kind also had the kind of features that artists adored.

Because of his work, he knew her records and personal history like the back of his hand. Her bare foot, though, was new.

She was natural and earthy, this woman who had become an unexpected obsession and the future mother of his child.

The image she presented asleep fit the setting like a perfect peg—a Renaissance beauty in classic repose inside a sixteenth-century farmhouse with huge aged beams, a picturesque thatch roof and happy little farm critters. It was at least as ideal a setting for her as standing as the knight in blue armor in front of the queen. She oozed tradition and old-fashioned values. It shouldn't have captivated him. It was boring. And yet, here he was.

That she could inhabit each space so fluently was a quiet marvel to him. Jenna was natural wherever she was because she brought the characteristic of naturalness to everything she did.

What must it be like to walk into any arena and be so easily loved? He would have to add it to the short list of things he didn't know.

He had imagined she would be a T-shirt and panty type rather than a pretty nightgown type, but he appreciated the unexpected. There was more *feminine* and *wild* and *free* blended into the *good* and *honest* and *upright* in her than he had realized at first glance.

Jenna had a unique way of surprising him at every turn.

It was the special light she had, the lack of self-consciousness that was so unlike anything else he'd ever encountered throughout his jaded life.

It blinded him every time he came near.

And he'd gone and gotten caught up staring at her after all, he observed wryly.

She stirred, subconsciously sensing his presence, even while she remained asleep.

He had moved to wake her, silently repositioning himself at her bedside, when she sat up suddenly in bed.

"Sebastian?" she asked groggily. Her voice was sleepy and sweet and confused. Here, at least, was a surprise he could use to his advantage.

He sat down on the bed beside her. "Present," he said.

"What are you doing here? How did you get in?"

Only truth worked with Jenna.

"I'm here because you're pregnant."

He had not expected that she would leap back from him into a defensive posture, but supposed he really should have. She was a security professional.

"Who are you?" Her voice had become fully

alert and dropped into her lower register, full of fearless menace.

Lifting his hands, palms up, he kept his voice even as he replied, "Relax, Jenna. We have a lot to talk about."

Her eyes narrowed, shadowed and cold. "Who are you?"

"You know who I am, Jenna," he soothed.

She bared her teeth.

He gave her what she wanted. "I'm Sebastian Redcliff. I am also the Director of Central Intelligence."

She wasn't buying it. "Cyrano doesn't have Central Intelligence," she countered, losing none of her defensiveness.

He gave her a half smile. "Not officially."

Her ferocity popped like a balloon at his words, leaving her collapsed against the bed with her hands over her face in its wake. The information was new, but he imagined it answered too many of her unanswered questions to deny.

"I'm such a fool," she said softly.

It wasn't the first time someone had said the words as a result of a conversation with him, but he hated the weary self-recrimination in her voice.

"For not knowing national secrets?" he asked softly.

"I work in national security."

"Exactly why you shouldn't know. It'd be a

disaster if the front staff knew about what went on in the back of house. Otherwise, how would it sound genuine when you insisted to the public that Cyrano has no intelligence program?"

Their breathing and heartbeats were the only sounds for a moment.

Then she let out a dry, joyless laugh and said, "We had sex."

"We did. We're consenting adults, it's not against the law. Or did you mean you expected to know through some kind of sex osmosis?"

"You're a complete stranger." She sounded horrified at herself, as if she had lost herself in the woods.

Reaching toward her, he took her hand. In truth, she was taking his revelation well. "Get to know me, then. Come to Redcliff with me. Stay there throughout your pregnancy. I will take care of you and our baby and you can meet the father of your child."

She scoffed. "If that's even possible. Do you let anyone know you?"

He didn't, but strangely it stung to hear her say so when she was the one person he'd made the offer to. "No," he said.

She sat up again slowly.

A long silent beat passed during which she stared at him, a dusky rose blush blossoming across her cheeks. "You could have called. Or even come by during normal visiting hours."

Eyes locked on hers, he shook his head. "You would have ignored me or had your mother tell me you were sick."

She sucked in a breath at his words, her glorious chest lifting and pausing there, her body gone rigid at his accurate summation. "You tapped my phone."

He didn't bother to deny it. "Years ago, when you applied for a position on the royal guard."

"That's appalling."

He shook his head. "No. It's intelligence. Unless you're suggesting we let just anyone become a royal guard?"

She laughed again and though it remained a sarcastic sound, this time it carried some amusement.

"None of us knew," she said.

He nodded graciously. "Thank you. I take pride in my work."

"Helene?" she asked.

"Not even the famous duchess guard knows."

"But she has the highest-level security clearance."

He quirked a brow up. "Does she?"

Jenna laughed again, light and full for its low volume, and the sound soothed something unsettled within him.

"You broke into my room," she pointed out.

He nodded. "I did, and at great peril to myself, as you're one of the most dangerous women in the nation."

She smiled, as he'd intended, and he felt the same thrill of accomplishment he did after co-ordinating a successful intelligence mission.

But soon her smile faded, her eyebrows coming together before another long moment passed in silence. Then she said, shaking her head, "I can't believe I just took it all at face value."

She still felt like a fool, that was obvious, but she no longer hated herself for it.

It was an improvement at least.

Then she said, "This makes you my boss, you know. I could sue you."

He stared at her blankly for a moment before he chuckled. "That's a new reaction."

"To?"

"To learning my job title."

"I should hope this is a new situation," she said primly. "You could have called or sent an email. You didn't have to break into my house."

"Your parents' house."

"My home."

He looked around, noting the girlish decor, the discrete boxes of items that obviously did not belong to her, were merely being stored in a space that was rarely occupied. "Your *childhood* home. You might have put your clothes back in the closet, but you don't live here."

"Your parents' house is always your home," she countered.

He looked at her pityingly. "Is it?"

Instead of fire, sympathy flashed across her eyes. "It's supposed to be."

Irritated by the unintended shift in subject, he waved her off. "I didn't come here to discuss our parents. I came here to discuss us as parents."

Her abruptly tired eyes narrowed as she tilted her head to one side, her arms coming to cross in front of her stomach in a protective position. "So talk."

"We have a lot to go over."

"So you broke into my house in the middle of the night?"

"It was the only way I could be sure of reaching you. You left the capital and have refused every call from there—barring the single instance of contact you had with Helene d'Tierrza upon her return—including three calls directly from the palace."

"As the head of intelligence, do you personally take such a close interest in all of the severance monitoring?"

He could appreciate that she was as intelligent as she was good, even while she challenged him. "Absolutely not, that would be ludicrous. 'Severance monitoring,' as you so eloquently put it, is normally rookie work. But I have never encountered anything with the power to distract me that you have, Jenna. You fascinate me. And that was before I learned you were carrying my child."

He spoke the truth.

Honesty was his only course with Jenna. And yet every time, he was left holding his breath and waiting for her response. It wasn't a particularly welcome sensation.

For another long stretch of heartbeats, she said nothing, only stared. Then she sighed, long and slow. Then she nodded.

"I'll go with you," she said.

The breath that had stuck in his chest eased free. "Thank you, Jenna."

"I've got to get my bags and leave a note," she groused.

"What will you tell them?"

"My mother knows about the baby. I'm just going to tell her the truth, that I've gone with the baby's father to sort things out."

Of course, she would tell the truth. Jenna valued it as much as he did, though she rarely weaponized it.

She stuffed a bag full of clothes and wrote a longer note than Sebastian had anticipated, but soon they were heading through the window.

As she went through before him, he asked, "Can you manage?"

Lifting an eyebrow, she said cockily, "With my eyes closed."

Smiling, he followed her through the window carrying her bag, feeling lighter than he had upon entry even with the extra weight. He hadn't been sure she would go with him.

He didn't know what he would have done had she refused. Seduction was no longer an option, not when he'd resolved to resist the dangerous attraction that remained between them, and he could not bodily force her.

It was fortunate, then, that he had not needed to devise an alternative. The fact that he felt the relief of that acutely, as if it were a matter of luck that things had gone smoothly, was a testament to how perilously footed he became when dealing with Jenna.

But if it emphasized the danger of getting closer to her, it also showed that he could navigate the thin middle way. He had underestimated her allure in thinking a single taste would render her harmless, but he had learned from his mistakes.

He would not touch her again, would not feed the hunger that he could now recognize as the same kind of obsession that had driven his father. Instead, they would work together to give their child the kind of childhood that produced a soul like Jenna's. Jenna had earned his trust long ago—enough to appoint her to the most important security detail in the nation. She would be an excellent mother. He would keep them safe and provide them with what they needed.

They moved in silence to where he had parked his Trevita a distance from her house. The sleek and stealthy car was a ghost gray that was a one-of-a-kind deviation from the extremely limited three-car run that the greater public knew about. The King of Sweden had gifted Sebastian the rare car as a thank-you for information services rendered and it was stealth incarnate.

"Nice car," Jenna said, a little breathless at its passenger side. Her tongue came to her lips, wetting them, as they took in the vehicle, and the eroticism of her perusal hit him like an invisible wall.

At a glance, the car looked like a standard luxury sports model, as common as any slate-gray Lamborghini. Upon closer examination, however, the infinite superiority of its craftsmanship was evident in every gorgeous fiber of its diamond-weave exterior. It wasn't paint that gave it its distinctive color and texture, but strands of woven carbon fiber. The handling was so responsive that he felt like he could drive it with his mind—a pleasure that was almost as unique as Jenna.

He was grateful for it for more practical reasons tonight, however. He was also appreciative of the moonless night above. The vehicle had been made to move invisibly through a night like this. But tonight, what had pleased him the most about the car was the way Jenna's eyes lit up when they'd landed on it.

Its top speed was outrageous for Cyrano, but tonight he would get close to it, if only to please the gearhead he suspected lurked beneath Jenna's exterior.

The journey passed quickly enough that they left the picturesque country lane in a blur.

A drive that should have taken him forty-five minutes took him twenty, and just as he'd planned, between the vehicle's color and the darkness, and the speed, no one saw him as he took the long dark road to the Redcliff estate. He didn't want to deal with the fanfare of arriving during regular hours.

The forbidding wrought iron gated entrance to the walled estate opened for him, the massive *R* in their center splitting to welcome the prodigal son home.

Named not for seaside cliffs, as most assumed, Redcliff was landlocked, located to the northeast of the seaside capital, so-called because of the high, clay-rich cliffs that slashed through the center of its boundaries, carved into the countryside over thousands of years by the Soleil River.

As they climbed the curving road that followed the river at an incredible height toward the main residence, the shocking cliffs were invisible in the darkness. Just as was each and every one of the other small details about Redcliff that generally never failed to bring a smile to his cynical mouth. The vibrant green of the grassy hills and clifftops, all the more luminous for the contrast of the red soil beneath. The trees packed together in dense patches and groves sporadically dotted across the landscape, clinging to the hills for dear life. The faded brown brick and terra-cotta tiled rooftops of the village homes. The structures lined the roadway, tight together, often so close they touched, built atop and into the sturdiest of the cliffs, connected by families, clotheslines, Wi-Fi passwords and busy lives.

He couldn't remember the last time he'd come to Redcliff. Possibly not since his last annual tour.

Too long.

At the top of the cobblestone drive was the ducal complex. Neither a manor nor a palace, the Redcliff compound was a sleek and contemporary structure that had been designed to blend seamlessly into the landscape. Boasting the very best of every modern convenience, with everything tastefully built into the structure itself, the luxurious space ensured that one could remain entirely connected to the world while feeling absolutely free from human society.

He knew this because he was responsible for its design.

Tearing down the old manor—a stately and stiff monstrosity that had been drafty, sat uncomfortably with its modern additions, and was haunted by memories of his mother and father's failures—had been his first act when he'd taken over the title upon his father's death.

He had been younger then, still passionate about architecture, before he'd realized that even a perfectly designed house did not make a home.

He had thought it would somehow change his memories of Redcliff if he replaced the house, that it would eradicate the persistent sense of isolation which dogged him every time he climbed the hill from the village and saw the ancestral grounds come into view.

He had been young and wrong, but the complex he had built was beautiful.

Elegant and comfortable, it had been designed for a family, a thing he could admit now that it was on its way to becoming a reality, but stepping inside with Jenna at his side, her bag slung over his shoulder, he realized immediately why it had always remained so cold.

Jenna had never been here.

And because she was with him, it felt profoundly different when he crossed the threshold this time.

He didn't know if it was because she carried his child or simply because she transformed every space she entered with her presence, but her magic was working already, her wide-eyed wonder at his creation finally proving his youthful idealism right.

His creation could become a home.

The glass entry doors slid open silently, admitting her like a temple goddess, the movement of air their motion caused strangely worshipful.

They strolled down hallways that appeared to be open air but were truly cleverly laid-out indoor spaces, perfectly climate-controlled in a way a stroll through the surrounding hillsides would never be, and she trailed her fingertips delicately along the gleaming wooden handrails while gazing at the outer world. He felt her touch as if she caressed his skin rather than his design.

Did she appreciate that he had made nature into a performance? Did she know that he had never invited anyone into his private project until her, that she was the sole audience he had intended to impress without ever knowing? He only realized it himself now.

He led her to the bedroom that was nearest to his office—near enough that he would hear her if she needed anything.

"I thought you would like this room."

It took her a moment of looking inside, mouth slightly ajar, before she turned back to him. "Thank you. We never talked about—"

He shook his head, anticipating her concern. "My room is in another part of the house. My office, however, is next door should you need anything. I'm in there most often."

"About the baby—"

"Tomorrow," he forestalled her. "When we're fresh. Make yourself comfortable. There's a private bathroom adjacent."

She looked at him, brown eyes serious, and opened her mouth as if she wanted to say something but then closed it with a shake of her head. "Thank you. Good night, Sebastian."

He tried to stick this image of her in his mind, as she was now, a lovely woman in a virginal nightgown, as opposed to the version of her performing erotic dances that had filled it as of late. Her proximity would be a challenge but perhaps in easing into a daily routine with her, one populated with encounters comprised of mundane pleasantries and virginal nightgowns, he could conquer the dangerous desire. "Good night, Jenna."

Leaving her there to settle in, he made his way to his office. Along the way, he passed the high wall of family portraits.

Comfort, aesthetics and a grudge against his parents might have motivated his youthful renovation of the homestead, but beyond that, he didn't bear any ill will toward his family history.

He was proud of it, in fact.

He certainly appreciated the fact that it made him rich.

Despite the renovation, he had saved the paintings and various heirlooms, even going so far as to preserve a stained-glass window from the oldest portion of the original structure.

The design of the window was simple and lovely, a white lily at its focal point, the petals of which were shapes cut from three types of glass—an opaque white, a mottled and sparkling translucent, and a softly transparent ivory. Brassy burned-orange glass for a stamen and pale sage for the leaves completed the image, which was surrounded and framed by an array of assorted translucent blues and greens.

It was the cliff lily of his family crest, and the first stained-glass window ever brought to the island of Cyrano, even before the island had become a unified nation. The Redcliff family was a part of Cyrano's history, at least as much as the royal family and its relations. His family had been the spark and ember of what would later become a rich and artistic cultural tradition.

Sebastian had studied stained glass for months, practicing restoration techniques on the rose in the d'Tierrza library before he dared preserve and move the Redcliff lily. It was one of the reasons that he had become so familiar with the d'Tierrza library in the first place. Why it was his most treasured location for meetings in the capital.

At the thought of the library, his mind, of course, turned to Jenna.

It seemed all roads led to Jenna and the child she carried, no matter what direction he turned.

It was fortunate, then, that he had the power to redraw the map so that every one of them ended where he wanted.

CHAPTER EIGHT

THE BEDROOM SEBASTIAN had given her was incredibly beautiful.

Large rectangular paneled windows offered a stunning panoramic view from where she sat in the center of a massive bed. The bed itself, covered in stark white plush downy bedding, jutted out from a wood-slatted wall that supported it, appearing to float in the air.

In addition to the bed, a number of various-sized flat and cubed shelves were arranged tastefully along the slats. They boasted vibrant potted plants, decorative sculptures and books. There were no photos but, though she'd looked, she hadn't really expected to find any. She did not picture Sebastian as the family photo type.

Sliding her legs out of the bed, Jenna slowly stood.

Blessedly, her stomach remained where it was supposed to be.

Between her pregnancy and the effect Sebastian had on her system, she was grateful for any moment she felt steady. She felt like herself for this moment, and she would take it. Her baby and her onetime lover both seemed happy to engage in a constant battle for supremacy inside her consciousness, and the opportunity to anchor down and hold on to herself, even briefly, was a deep relief.

They had yet to discuss the details of their arrangement, but it was obvious to Jenna that reining in the out-of-control flares of attraction between them would be of paramount importance.

Giving in to those urges, that lunacy, really, had wreaked enough havoc in their lives. And more than that, she couldn't afford the risk of losing herself in him again.

Digging inside her old academy duffel bag, she grabbed the first dress that came to hand—a bright red loose-fitting linen maxi dress with three-quarter-length sleeves that her mother had made for her years ago.

It was voluminous and airy, intended to be worn at the end of summer when the family could spend entire days in the heat, preparing and storing their annual harvest.

With the right layering, she could wear it through a chill morning, the heat of the afternoon and into the coolness of the evening comfortably. It was practical, as well as lovely and durable, just like everything her mother made.

After dressing, she headed through the door Sebastian had indicated was the bathroom.

Like the bedroom, the bathroom boasted large landscape-view windows that looked out over the incredible rust-colored cliff sides that surrounded the building, but when it came to focal pieces, the bathroom put even the bedroom to shame.

A gorgeous wooden tub—huge, square and deep, and a smooth, creamy honey color that a high-end hair salon would have been proud of—was raised in the center of the room. The inner lining of the tub was made from what looked like smooth gray stone, the same material from which the sinks appeared to have been made. Rather than a traditional faucet, the tub could be filled via a large wooden spigot, controlled by a pull chain with a matching wooden handle.

Jenna had seen many examples of astounding luxury over her life as a royal guard, but this bathroom was by far the best marriage of wealth and design that she had ever encountered.

Bringing herself to leave the bathroom to find Sebastian was hard, especially after discovering the shower alcove with its scandalous full-length cliff window—a complete outdoor shower experience without ever leaving the house. In exchange, all you had to do was bare your naked self to the entirety of the natural world.

She could not help but suck in a slow breath, in awe at the audacity and appeal of the space.

Without having to be told, it was clear to her that Sebastian had designed the house. It was just like him—breathtakingly audacious.

The man was an absolute hedonist.

As if the thought brought him to life, she caught a whisper of his scent in the air. Backtracking the way she had come, forcibly ignoring the artistry and details of the walls, she looked for him in the room he'd labeled his office the night before.

Upon entry, she gasped aloud.

Inside, the sprawling space overlooked the Soleil River. Cherry-stained built-in bookshelves spanned the length of the wall to her left at the doorway, but it was the desk that stole her breath.

It was centered in an entirely glass-walled space that was cantilevered out boldly over the river's deep ravine, seemingly with no support beneath its gleaming hardwood floor. The desk itself was large and heavy, parked with authority on the gorgeous rug that lay in the center of the hardwood. To preside as duke in situ here was to be king of the sky—to conquer the raging elements, to survey and command all that the light touched and more.

It was awe-inspiring and terrifying at the same time.

The rest of the office, the part that behaved like a normal room, was dominated by gleaming cherry woods and smooth leather. The contrast, everything right and proper that one might imagine in a traditional office on the one hand, and terrifyingly futuristic on the other, somehow screamed both conflict and triumph, and Jenna wondered what battle it was that Sebastian was fighting through the space.

With a start, she realized she'd been standing there at the entryway gazing in astonishment at an empty room.

She'd never been interested in decorating or design, but it was impossible not to be while inside Redcliff. It was the most incredible home she'd ever entered, a masterful work of art that revealed Sebastian's signature style, his passion and sensuousness, with every brushstroke.

Leaving the room, she went in the opposite direction, retracing last night's steps down the long skywalk that was even more enchanting in its integration with the outside world by daylight than it had been the night before. Between what felt like the miles of windows and the vibrant tropical potted plants, the walk felt more like a summer stroll than a passage to the front door.

She followed the way down the long hall until she stepped out into the large open living area that they had passed through the night before. Empty of Sebastian too, this room, while impeccably decorated and obviously to the highest taste, was almost disappointing in its normalcy. Even with its elegance, it was just a place to watch television, nothing like the bathroom and bedroom and office she'd seen.

She followed the flow of the architecture around a bend and partial wall to step into a home chef's wonderland.

Like the bedroom she had woken up in, the enormous chef's kitchen faced out toward the cliffs, with a wall of windows providing a panoramic view from pretty much every potential cooking and preparation area.

An enormous kitchen island dominated the center of the room, situated in front of a massive range and oven that were equipped with a restaurant hood.

The sink was sunken into the island and everywhere else was clear, open counter space—miles of it, in fact. The glossy marble was thick and ivory colored with a subtle beige pattern. None of the standard countertop appliances one might expect marred the clean expanse. She suspected that they existed in abundance, however, but were merely hidden amongst the myriad of unique custom cabinets.

As incredible as it was, however, what struck her most about the grandiose kitchen was that it was made to be cooked in. It wasn't a showpiece, and it wasn't a sterile professional workspace tucked away from view where the staff worked like in many of the homes of the super-wealthy she had visited in service to the queen.

This kitchen was meant to be the place where the people who called the place home gathered and created memories.

It was the height of luxury, and yet it was also somehow normal—wholesome, even—and to find it right smack-dab in the middle of the home of one of Cyrano's wealthiest aristocrats and oldest families… Jenna would not have expected it.

Even more astounding, Sebastian leaned against the counter, fingers deftly typing something into his phone.

In the kitchen's morning light, which was extensive and bright since this room—like all the others she had been inside—had floor-to-ceiling panoramic landscape windows, he looked fresh and handsome. Certainly nothing like the kind of man who might sneak into your room and ask you to run away from home. Nor did he particularly look like the kind of man who might ask you to make love with him in a library.

Instead, he was tan and tall and green-eyed, his blond hair tidy, his jeans and button-up relaxed despite the fact that everything he wore was perfectly tailored to his long, lean frame. He was stunning and wealthy in equal measure—the kind of man who could look impeccably put together with almost no effort—but here in his own kitchen he was approachable, just a regular man somehow, as if this were an ordinary morning and she were just now joining him for breakfast after spending extra time luxuriating in bed.

The vision her eyes presented was all a lie, though. It had to be. The aura of normalcy that clung to him, the way that coming upon him in the morning felt more comfortable than even returning to her own childhood home—none of that coincided with the enigmatic denizen she knew from the city.

But she didn't really know him at all, did she?

She was going to have to get that through her head before she did something even more foolish than she already had with him. Coming with him had been about getting to know the father of her child, not falling for a man she'd had no business being with in the first place. And certainly not on the first day.

Shaking her head, she chastised herself mentally.

He looked about as normal as Adonis masquerading as a human man, and the sense of comfort and rightness was just her hormones and desires switching on at the sight of a man she was obviously infatuated with.

A mother didn't let those kinds of urges guide her, though. Particularly not when the man in question wanted everything his way and was good at making it happen.

Armed with the reminder, she dared look again.

His jeans were a dark wash and at their base, his high-quality leather work boots looked supple from use and care.

She had never seen him in jeans and boots.

Did wealthy city people wear jeans and boots? Only eight weeks from living in the palace and it seemed she couldn't remember any of the wealthy people she had ever seen.

There was only Sebastian.

His shirt was a buttery-soft green flannel, a shade darker than his jaded dragon eyes.

All but the top button of his shirt were closed. There was nothing seductive about the shirt, and yet her mouth watered. His unexpectedly muscled forearms felt indecent, revealed by his rolled-up sleeves.

She sucked in an audible breath, her resolutions forgotten in the face of the full power of him in the light of day.

He looked up from the device in his hand.

Their eyes locked and the jolt of electricity and understanding was as bad as it always was, worse even.

Attraction was not what lived between them. The word was too soft and flirty. Whatever it was that existed between them was thick and demanding and relentless. They hooked into one another and squeezed and tangled like ivy until she was sure they would both be lost in a vortex of green.

He stole her breath, her body instantly coming alive, making her wish she'd chosen something else besides the airy dress to wear—twelve layers of something else.

The same intensity of need burned in his stare, perhaps ever greater now than it had that day in the library, the dangerous green orbs dancing with the shapes of all the dirty things it was clear he still wanted to do to her.

Searching for the frayed strands of her intentions with no luck and irritated by everything delicious and fascinating about him, she snapped, "Good morning."

He laughed and she was momentarily mesmerized. "Good morning. Did you sleep well?"

She hadn't, but that wasn't for lack of comfort so she was polite when she said, "Yes, thank you. And you?"

His eyes lit with mischief. "Well, thank you. Can I interest you in something to drink, Jenna? I've got a number of options. Ginger lemonade?" He should never have been able to pull off mild mannered and charming, and yet here he was.

"That's sounds wonderful, actually. Thank you."

He got the glass for her himself, and when he turned to return the lemonade to the refrigerator, she was filled with a longing for this all to be about the energy that still sizzled between them rather than making arrangements for their unborn child.

But that wasn't for women like her. She was a sidekick, not a main character.

She took a sip and steadied herself. The lemonade was fresh and delicious, exactly the thing her stomach had been searching for as her occupied system woke up.

"Your home is astounding. I feel a little out of place," she admitted.

"You shouldn't, someday your child will own it."

He said it so casually, completely nonchalant, as if he was entirely comfortable with the sudden redirection of his life and permanence of their bond. Perhaps he was?

It was taking her longer to adjust.

Hollowly, she wondered where she would fit into the life of a child who would one day own Redcliff. It didn't compute that that child and her child would be one and the same. Would they be embarrassed that she was so obviously not from their world?

She would have to work and wait for the answer, like everything else in her life.

Regardless, there had been something warm and tender about Sebastian's words. He had a gift for making it difficult for her to see the lines that separated her from the world she now walked through.

"I've downloaded your checkup schedule and updated your records with your new address and my emergency contact information."

Jenna gasped. "That's completely inappropriate, you know. The public would be horrified to know you could access that kind of information."

With complete seriousness he responded, "You're absolutely right, and because of that, I am going to have to ask you to keep the information to yourself. I know I can trust you, of course. You've taken an oath to protect and serve."

"Those are pretty words after you've already risked state secrets."

He squeezed her shoulder, the contact lighting the smoldering flame inside her. "I have absolute faith in you," he said.

He meant it, and he was right to trust her. They might be strangers, and yet in so many ways he knew her, understood her.

She couldn't say the same about him, though.

And chipping away at that imbalance was just one of the Herculean tasks she had to accomplish during her time with him.

"You know more about me than I know about you," she said aloud.

"I know more about most people than they know about me."

"Most people are not going to be the mother of your children."

A moment of silence greeted her statement before he said, "Agreed."

"So, I should know you."

"I am unknowable," he said.

Jenna snorted. "Only God is unknowable. Tell me about yourself."

He sighed, sounding bored. "What do you want to know?"

She shrugged, sipping at her lemonade. "What do you love? What's your favorite color? Only the truth." She pictured her questions landing on him like birds, beginning as a singleton then building into a flock.

Beside her he stilled. His eyes narrowed, scanning her, while the wheels of his mind turned. When he spoke, less than a heartbeat later, he answered her questions in rapid-fire succession, though she knew he'd thoroughly processed and controlled just what he would reveal.

"I love knowing things other people don't and the color of your eyes," he said, his words rough where before they had been cultured and smooth.

Once again, he'd floored her with the truth. Multiple truths, in fact.

Each one was meaty, too much to take in at a time, let alone in rapid succession. Especially since he had moved behind her and threaded his fingers through her hair to massage her scalp.

His fingers were gentle though she sensed annoyance coiled in his touch.

He didn't want to share with her, even as he endeavored to open.

His fingers were strong and deft and she couldn't help the quiet moan that escaped, even as she sensed she should keep the evidence of her weakening will private—for both of their sakes. But she didn't, and in response, he let out a sound of frustration before tilting her head up and taking her lips in a kiss that was soft and restrained for all of the denied passion clamoring behind it.

When he pulled back, slow and lingering, she held still for a moment, savoring the thing that shouldn't have happened—lips parted, eyes closed—before she opened her eyes with a frown.

"Sebastian, we can't—"

A strange expression came to his face—intense, needy and deep—but flickered away before he pulled away from her to say, "You're right, of course."

"We should talk about—" she started.

"Not yet," he said, voice taut, expression mildly pained. His nostrils flared as he drew in a long, slow breath. "Space. A change of scenery. I have something I want to show you," he said.

"What?" she asked, her body still yearning toward his while her mind did its best to pull everything back in after their slip.

"The rest of the house," he said. "I designed it."

Grateful for the obvious diversion, Jenna jumped on it, exclaiming, "I suspected that!" And it wasn't even work to force a smile at the confirmation. Though there was a sin in pride, it felt good to be right after such a long spell.

Her bruised instincts were grateful for the vindication.

When he spoke again, it was a beat too late and only after he'd cleared his throat and taken her hand. "This way."

The rest of Redcliff was as astounding as the small portion she had seen.

As she'd expected, Sebastian had stamped himself everywhere.

Shadows played everywhere, lovely and peaceful, while the materials he'd chosen and natural light through the various slatted shoji walls and abundance of stunning cliff-view windows ensured that light was always available to create them.

She said as much as he led her through, her voice tinged with awe, as he led her around. "I understand the light, everyone wants natural light, but I would have never imagined how shadows could be used to enhance a room."

Another odd expression sparked across his

face at her words, but he only said, "It's observant of you to notice. Not many do," before showing her the next wondrous delight.

Every room was astounding. He had an incredible, high-tech conference room, separate from his office. There was a workout room with fantastic equipment. At one end of the incredible home, two stories had been built around the tallest tree Jenna had ever seen on the island of Cyrano.

As a former royal guard, Jenna had entered some of the most extravagant and expensive houses in the world, but this was the first to make her wish she had the kind of money to create something like it for herself.

Through Sebastian's clever design, the mansion was situated and arranged so that nearly every room he showed her included an astonishing cliff view.

The stunning and rugged rust-colored terrain, the dramatic drop and roar of the river—all of it did far more to trumpet just whose home this was than any stodgy coat of arms ever could.

Like Sebastian, the Redcliff estate was too powerful to be subtle and was utterly unconcerned with pretending otherwise.

But if you like the view, her inner romantic purred, sliding itself out of the corner she thought she'd beaten it back to, *it's perfect*.

After he'd shown her far more rooms than she

expected there to be in one house, he tugged her just a bit farther into the fully shadowed part of a hallway, where she was surprised to see another door.

"Another room?"

"One of my favorites," he said.

Reflecting on the glorious rooms he'd just shown her, she was skeptical that it would outdo them. "It's got a lot to live up to."

He replied mysteriously, "I think you'll find it as arresting as I do."

When he opened the door, she sucked in a breath, her cheeks flaming at the same time.

Inside was a library.

Smaller than the one that was now burned into her memory, Sebastian's library was a cozy, plush and private sanctuary. Each and every book boasted a cracked spine and a siren allure, enticing, calling to its reader. Scanning the titles proved that though new, the collection was as eclectic and broad as any discerning reader might desire.

Whereas the d'Tierrza library had emphasized many reading nooks, this cozy room was centered around a decadent central space, arranged as if intended for a group of readers to gather and quietly read together. A sofa, two large cushioned armchairs, and two large floor cushions encircled a luxurious Turkish rug, each seating area equipped with a small table beside it and a bevy of pillows and cushions. What-ever position a person might desire to take, they could achieve it with the plethora of options, each one designed to accommodate the plea-sure of reading.

Or making love, she added to her mental observations, her body near combustion with sensual overload and determined to once again break down her common sense.

If the d'Tierrza library had been built for show, the Redcliff library had been built to be used and enjoyed, and not just by anyone, but Sebastian—and, she realized with a start, her eyes landing on the one bay of shelves filled with new books, their spines unbroken, her.

He'd been awfully confident she would come with him.

The assumption that the new books were for her trickled into certainty as the titles in the collection began to sink in. They covered sub-jects she had excelled in at the academy, as well as those she had not done as well in, but main-tained an interest in. He'd included popular fic-tion titles she'd been meaning to check out by authors she'd bought before. She was impressed by his selection. He might have access to the best intel in the country, but it was another thing entirely to pick out a book for someone.

But of greater interest to her than even the excellent books he'd selected for her were the ones he had chosen for himself through the years.

Those were fascinating for a whole different reason—for what they revealed about him.

He watched her silently as she walked along the shelves reading titles, running her fingers along shelves and up and down spines.

Language, foreign policy, world history, politics and—of course—architecture, dominated.

Was it any wonder he was interested in espionage?

Though it made sense that it would take quite a lot of study to know so much that he had no business knowing, she was impressed by the amount of time he spent continuing to learn.

It was an admirable thing to do, far more so than many of the other things she'd witnessed wealthy people do with their free time.

In front of the reading area, a massive fireplace, already set with logs for a fire, sat quietly.

He had outdone himself with the house, but it was this secret inner garden that slipped past the defenses she had erected around her heart.

He had created space out of time, and welcomed her into it—and this time, there was a lock on the door.

Whatever they got up to in this oasis, there was no chance they would be interrupted.

In the face of all the emotion, all she could say was, "Very bold of you."

He smiled with one side of his mouth. "I think we've established that."

She did her best to remember to be professional, to recall that she didn't need to want this man. She needed to get to know him, she needed to work together with him to plan a future for her child. This wasn't about them.

It wasn't about the memories and sensations flooding her mind and body, returning her to a different library.

She wanted him even more now.

He wanted her even more now.

Their shared desire was as unspoken as their agreement to resist it. She sensed that though they came to the decision for individual reasons, they were at least as in sync about this consensus as they were physically.

They had so much to do, so much to plan and learn about each other and the world they would build for their child.

They wanted the same things, even the ones they couldn't have.

Her brown eyes locked on his green.

He was beautiful—slightly amoral or not.

She was far past being able to tell which he was, only that a part of her was convinced he was hers.

Either way, it didn't matter. He fascinated her.

Like magnets, they stepped toward one another, erasing the space between them in synchronized movements, as if greater powers had choreographed them.

He opened his mouth.

She licked her lips.

His eyes locked on the motion, and he swallowed.

"The baby," she said.

He nodded. "We need to talk about the baby."

She nodded, heat rising to her cheeks, her skin tingling and alert. "First and foremost."

The tension between them stretched tight, egged on by the heat, and the sumptuous library, and the man she had already proven she was willing to risk everything to touch.

And then he was closing the space between them on a strangled oath, his arms coming around her.

Jenna sighed into his mouth as he took hers, her body weeping with the relief of giving in and the end of the tension of resisting her attraction to him.

Her body was a cascade of needs, a rush of wanting him that demanded everything all at once—sensitive, hot and famished.

She wanted to bite him, wanted to savor him and wanted him inside her, ravishing and soft and gentle, all at the same time. The immensity of the conflict came out as a growl against his lips, which, devil that he was, only made him smile.

The experience of kissing him the first time had been an awakening, and earlier, in the kitchen, a dreamy whisper. Now, it was an incendiary, sparking a fire he'd built deep inside her, her skin flushed hot and her nerve endings blossoming into sensitivity greater than she knew what to do with.

She was transcendent, the incredible rushes of pleasure leaving her desperate for more, holding on to her form as long as it took for the entire universe to break apart.

When his hand cupped her breast over the thin, soft fabric of her dress, she moaned into his mouth. As if the sound had aggravated him beyond control, he swept her into his arms before carrying her to the sofa, where he lay her down, never breaking their kiss.

Her hands explored his chest and shoulders, adoring the softness of his sweater against them as they trailed toward the hemline. There, she slipped her fingers beneath the fabric of his clothing to feel his hot skin pulsing beneath her hands.

His breath caught at contact, and a hot rush pulsed at her center. That this man, powerful enough that he could direct an international espionage program, trembled for her—plain, Priory Jenna—shook her to the core.

Abruptly hating that clothing separated them, Jenna pulled him close, driven by an urge to fuse with him that she knew he felt just as powerfully.

And then his pocket trilled, vibrating and ringing a jaunty tune absolutely out of place amidst the hungry sounds of their breathing.

Gasping, she looked around, momentarily disoriented as he pulled back to slip the device out of his pocket and hold it up. In that moment, he was disheveled and real and completely within her reach, his clothing off-kilter, and hair tousled where her fingers had run through it. And he looked as shaken as she was.

"It's the king. I have to take this," he said, distancing himself from her more effectively with the words than even the large steps away he took as he straightened his shirt and moved to answer.

It was as if a bucket of icy water had been spilled over her.

Jenna shivered, now cold where she had been on fire only moments before.

Incredibly, it seemed the king's reach extended even further than she had ever imagined. The monarch had somehow managed to insert himself into yet another shameful encounter with Sebastian, despite the fact that he was hours away and no longer her employer.

But, she thought, as she pulled herself back together, the sound of Sebastian's muted conversation low in the background, this time the interruption hadn't come too late, after things had already been said and done that couldn't be taken back. He had saved them from repeating that folly at least.

The last thing that she and Sebastian needed was to be intimate again.

They *needed* to sit down and have some serious conversations. They *needed* to hammer out their plan for parenting together.

The combustible attraction between them had only increased, but it would only burn them both. That was more clear than ever.

And none of that talking was going to happen in his sumptuous library. The two of them needed a less sensual space, a place where they wouldn't be tempted to explore anything other than the future of their child.

So, rather than wait for him to finish his business on the phone, Jenna gestured to excuse herself, ignored his motion to stay and made her way back to the kitchen to wait for him.

In a kitchen, with space between them, they would surely be able to talk.

CHAPTER NINE

HE HAD TO return to the capital.

Frustrated by the timing, even while acknowledging the summons had saved him from making a grave mistake, Sebastian hung up the phone and followed Jenna out of the library, knowing he would find her in the kitchen.

She was the hash-it-out-in-the-kitchen type.

It was simple and straightforward, unlike whatever information the king had for him, which could only be delivered in person.

Generally, this was the kind of information Sebastian lived for—secrets so big they could barely be uttered for fear of the consequences—but right now he had more important things on his mind.

Though perhaps the break and space would be blessings in disguise. Keeping his distance from her was proving more difficult than he'd anticipated, which only meant the threat she posed to him was greater. Clearly it would be a more challenging balancing act to walk and maintain the tightrope of his control while she remained within arm's reach.

Finding her in the kitchen, as he'd expected, he quickly briefed her. "I have to go to the capital. I'll be back tonight."

Shaking her head, she opened her mouth, likely to demand more of an explanation, but he held up a hand. "I'll tell you more later." It was a request.

That he stood to wait for her answer, that she had the power to say yes or no and have him obey when he allowed no one else that privilege irked him, but it was pointless to fight. She had it and he was completely at her mercy.

Finally, she relented with a short nod. "Fine. We need to talk, though."

"We do. Tonight," he promised, surprised to hear himself offering promises and more commitment than was necessary. Master of shadows and manipulation that he was, promises were something he didn't make lightly. He knew too well that promises were a form of honesty that could too easily be weaponized.

And as unusual as the promise was, what followed was even more so.

Turning to leave her there, he reached out to take her hand, absently, thinking nothing of the impulse, until his fingers grazed hers and caught.

Before he understood his intention, he had

snagged her arm, an echo of the afternoon of the gala, and spun her around to him. Drawing her closer, the movements as natural and fluid as they were foreign, he pressed a kiss first against her forehead, and then one to her lips, and then released her.

Only was it as he swept his phone from the countertop that he realized he'd kissed her goodbye, and only as he left Redcliff did he realize how good it had felt to have a reason to come home.

It was dark by the time he returned hours later than he'd anticipated.

Queen Mina was pregnant.

Babies, it seemed, were in the air and catching.

The information set off a strange mixture of reactions within him. Royal offspring and heirs were expected and Sebastian had protocols already established for the consequent expansion of his intelligence protection program required by their existence.

He had expected the news to be purely professional. He had known the monarch socially his entire life and had come to respect him immensely as a colleague and ruler, but he would not have said they were friends.

Never would he have imagined that, rather than a mild sense of pleasure that a man he liked had reason to celebrate, Sebastian's mind would instead jump to projections of future playmates for his child.

How would Jenna react?

How would she feel to know that the monarch was pregnant, as well? And Helene, too. Had she heard that her former partner was not only newly married, but had come back from her adventures pregnant, as well?

Yet again, Sebastian didn't know.

Driving into the garage and turning off the car, Sebastian noted as he got out and entered the house through the private door that he had spent more time at Redcliff in the past twenty-four hours than he had in the previous five years.

With Jenna in residence, the long drive between here and the capital seemed shorter.

To his pleasure, he found her back in the library, her legs curled up under her in one of the large chairs. A fire crackled cozily beside her.

"I lit the fire," she said, by way of greeting. Her voice was cool and tired, letting him know that she'd had a long time to circle around the topics at the top of her mind, including everything they still needed to discuss regarding their child.

Keeping his tone mild, he said, "I'm glad. You should make yourself at home."

She eyed him closely. "What did the king have to say?" she asked. She was probing, testing how much he could, or *would*, tell her.

The urge was there to share without reserve, so he hedged. "Let's take a walk," he said. She would come back to the question, he knew, but the invitation bought him time. Only Jenna seemed to have the ability to put him in the position of being short on said time.

She held his stare for a moment, those deep dark lances of hers piercing him without hesitation, and then nodded.

"There's a chill in the air outside," he said.

She flashed a small smile at his words, as if they'd surprised her. Walking past him, she said, "I'll grab a coat," leaving the room to, he presumed, retrieve her coat.

They met again in the kitchen, both of them somehow knowing that was where they would reunite.

He had installed her in his preferred bedroom, the one near his office, as opposed to the master suite, which he had taken, and he knew she knew the way.

In preparation for their walk, her attire was a study in contradictions.

She wore a long, tailored overcoat above her airy red dress and had matched it with a pair of floppy boots.

Together, the boots with the dress should not have worked—the style part country maiden, part grizzled dairy farmer—and yet it did, and somehow elegantly.

She brought the masculine and feminine, the sophisticated and the natural, into perfect balance effortlessly.

With her long braid, she looked entirely ready for a moonlit stroll in the countryside. Did he, he wondered, look as carefree and natural? Did he present the picture of a hearty and happy man of the landscape? Somehow, he doubted it. But he took her arm nonetheless, leading her outside through a side door that led into the woodland trails that constituted his landscaped forest garden.

Though they were here to discuss the future, one made infinitely more complicated by the intensity of the attraction that flared between them, walking through the moonlit woods with Jenna—even when that moon was little more than a thin sliver in the sky—came with a sense of peace that Sebastian had never experienced before.

The day with her had been a conflux of emotions, his control tenuous at best. At worst, well…at worst it had been the sweetness of kissing her in the kitchen and the inferno of touching her in the library.

Had he once again chosen the mistaken course with her? Should he have installed her somewhere other than Redcliff, at a more comfortable distance?

The idea offended both the father and the man

within him. He refused to keep any child of his at a comfortable distance and he had at least enough control to keep his hands to himself. Was that not one of the basic tenets of manhood?

The day's ups had been a testament to the strengths of his plan and the downs, merely a side effect of delaying this conversation too long.

Once they'd laid down parameters—one of which would be physical distance—neither would get carried away.

The trail ahead of them was lovely, wide and laid with a soft, sound-absorbent natural bedding of shredded bark. In the dim lighting, her hair shone like a raven's wing, her thick eyebrows drawn together making her look like a grave woodland witch from another era.

"What did the king say?"

What a strange thing it was to walk with Jenna in the woods.

Another woman might have gone immediately to the most pressing issue at hand—their baby—but not Jenna. She was a terrier and, though she continued to bafflingly rebut the idea, a professional.

Duty to the monarchs was more than a job to her, it was a part of her being. Her rejection of the reality of that—her rejection of the attempts that had been made to reinstate her to her position as guard—was the only lie he'd witnessed her utter.

Truth had always proven to be more powerful than lies, but he understood that people more often feared it than revered it. His father had belonged to that category of people.

But not Jenna. She had proven fearless in the face of the truth time and time again. He wondered what scary truth hid beneath the lie this time, but he did not ask. Now wasn't the time and if it was large enough to scare Jenna, it was best to approach with caution.

"The queen is pregnant," he finally answered her question.

Coming to an abrupt stop at his side, Jenna sucked in a hiss of air at the news, her hand coming to her abdomen in a protective gesture.

Ever the defender was Jenna, he observed, even when the heartache was her own.

"That's wonderful," she croaked thinly.

Eyeing her, he was ruthless, if only for her sake. "It's not. It hurts you to find out this way."

She winced, but did not deny it. "I'm happy for her."

He knew she told the truth, the way he always recognized truth when he heard it, but he could see that her joy for her friend was not strong enough to take away the sting.

An unfamiliar surge of irritation with the king rose in him. It was Sebastian's job to remain unequivocally in the king's corner, but in firing Jenna so impetuously, Zayn had made a huge mistake—and because that mistake had caused irreversible hurt to Jenna, it was an unforgiveable one.

But the queen, whom he knew thought of Jenna not just as an employee, but a true friend, had already told her husband as much before insisting that he retract his dismissal of her guard.

When the king had capitulated, however, and tried to rectify his mistake, Jenna had refused his calls, just as she had refused the queen's.

It took a lot of spunk to ignore a king's telephone calls. Sebastian had been proud of her.

But spunk didn't heal hurt feelings, and he suspected that what she needed was to talk to her friends.

While he excelled at planning in the shadows, he was powerless to address her current hurt. She had to take the first step.

More information, though, could potentially encourage the movement.

Information regularly inspired him to action, even when it hurt. Perhaps *especially* when it hurt.

"She is spending her pregnancy at the Summer Palace," he said.

Jenna nodded. "That makes sense. Will Hel accompany her?"

He could see the wheels of her mind turning. It was not customary for primary security to accompany the royal family to the summer palace, but the queen would miss her friends with such an extended stay.

Sebastian shook his head. "She will not. Helene is on maternity leave, as well."

"What?" Jenna's screech in reaction to the news was less reserved than it had been to the queen's. "But she—" She cut herself off before she revealed what he assumed was private information.

Idly intrigued, as he always was at the prospect of clandestine information, he set aside his curiosity at whatever barrier had previously existed to Helene having a child—a future that was somewhat expected of the head of one of the oldest families in the country—keeping his attention instead on Jenna.

When she finally spoke again, her voice was tired and quiet. "She didn't tell me."

Recalling the phone records he'd monitored, Sebastian said, "You only spoke once."

Jenna nodded. "Right after she got back. I was so glad she had returned safely, but when she tried to convince me to come back to the capital, I just couldn't. I cut her off and made an excuse to get off the phone. I never gave her a chance."

Although he had his own suspicions as to the answer, Sebastian asked, "Why?"

Jenna looked up at him, startled by the question. "I—" she started and stopped. Looking away, she said softly, "I don't belong there."

Had she not been serious, he would have scoffed. "You are one of the most qualified royal guards we have seen in over a decade, Jenna. Your service record is impeccable and you've only improved over the years."

She shook her head. "It's not about that. I'm invisible there, no one sees me," she said.

Lifting an eyebrow, he asked, "Isn't that what a guard is supposed to be?"

Again, she shook her head in a negative. "To the majority of people, yes. But not to everyone."

"I don't follow," he said, though he was beginning to understand.

"Helene has been my best friend for nearly a decade, and yet the gala was the first time I had ever been to her home. She and the queen have been the only people to see me, to be my friends in a real and meaningful way where I thought we were more than our roles, that we were the kind of close that opens and changes for each other, but neither of them shared their pregnancies with me."

"You haven't shared yours with them, either," he pointed out, happy to play devil's advocate if it meant presenting her with a more complete view of her situation. She was intelligent and savvy, but no one could truly see themselves.

Eyebrows drawing together in a frown, she waved her hand at him. "It's not the same."

"I think it might be closer than you think," he countered.

"No. It's not. They belong in that world. They understand the rules and where they fit. I thought I did too, but I was wrong."

"Aren't you the one who refused their calls?"

"Because they would only try to get me to come back," she said.

"Because you belong there," he pressed.

"I don't, Sebastian," she insisted. "Helene belongs there. She was born there and couldn't be invisible if she tried."

"And the queen?"

Jenna waved the point away. "She's the queen. She belongs wherever she wants."

"She wants you at her side."

"To be her friend on a payroll. What kind of friendship is that? What kind of real life? I wanted to join the rest of the world when I left my home for the capital, to find a place for myself amidst the bustle and noise. Well, the place I found was a background fixture and I don't want to continue consigning myself to that kind of echo of an existence. I thought I could have both and it turns out everyone else was right and I was wrong. I can live in the foreground of my life and be seen as a woman with value and skill if I'm willing to give up a career and get married like my Priory friends, or I can go back to the capital and return to being an interchangeable body in blue, only one that is pregnant with a new blemish on my record. That doesn't sound like belonging to me."

Like anyone in a spiral of shame and self-loathing—a mental and emotional cocktail Sebastian was intimately familiar with the signs of from the rare visits he'd had with his father throughout his childhood—she was painting a cherry-picked picture of her life to date, but he knew better than to point that out directly. "Being only the second woman appointed to the royal security force and graduating at the top of the military academy can hardly be considered an echo of an existence, Jenna."

"Of course, they can. Achievements don't constitute a life rich with love and warmth and laughter. Honors don't make a family or a home."

He raised an eyebrow, eyes darting pointedly to her abdomen. "Your condition contradicts that."

She made a noise in the back of her throat, hand once again protecting her belly, as if to shield their child from her next whispered words. "Pregnancy doesn't make a family, Sebastian."

He resisted the urge to laugh. She was correct. Pregnancy did not make a family. Attachment and dedication to one's children made a family, and—based on her self-censoring for the sake of baby ears that had not yet formed—he'd say she was more than halfway there already. To her, he said, "As I understand it, it does."

She shook her head. "Love makes a family."

Sebastian scoffed, mildly surprised to hear a woman as intelligent and down-to-earth as Jenna utter such a clichéd line. "Love makes people selfish and weak. A mother and father committed to their child's future make a family."

Distaste feathered her face. "That sounds like a business arrangement."

"We'd be lucky if more people took parenting so seriously," he countered, not exactly sure how they had gotten here from discussing her illusions.

"Well, why don't we get right to it then? Okay. I'm to assume you've got a number of proposals regarding the future of our offspring, then."

Irritation flared Sebastian's nostrils as he reminded himself that she would have no way of knowing that she mocked one of the great lessons of his life. As cherished and adored as Jenna must have been, she had no sense of what it was like to have parents with no plans, proposals, or even thoughts for their child.

"I do, most of which I'm sure we'll get to. We were, however, talking about your inane notions of not belonging."

She gasped in outrage. "Inane? Pardon me for noticing and caring when the people around me consider me a set piece."

"A set piece? I recognize the general cluelessness of most of the capital's citizenry, but that's a bit theatrical, Jenna."

Jenna scoffed. "Outside of the king and queen and Hel, I think you were the first person in the capital to ever see me."

Her words stoked his ego, but that would not soothe the hurt inside her, a hurt that was clearly older than the ones that lay between them. "I have to disagree, Jenna. Your work is admirable and noted. You were personally selected by the king to safeguard the queen. Your name is regularly cited as an example for the young girls of the nation. Put simply, you are remarkable, and it does not go unnoticed."

"I am not. I'm too Priory for the capital, and too capital for the Priory. To return to the palace is to accept a life without love and family and ordinary companionship. A life in which my most important relationships live and die at the whim of my employment. I want to build my own real home, rather than simply visit the one I grew up in on leave. I want to know the families of my closest friends and have their children call me Auntie, not Sergeant Moustafa. When I packed up my quarters alone after I was dismissed, I realized how truly little I had to show for the past decade of my life. My entire life fit into three boxes and there was no one there to say goodbye to me when I left. I don't want a life like that, where my presence or absence makes no difference. Even if leaving means giving up everything that I've dedicated myself to for the past two decades. All this time I thought I was following my dreams when it turns out I was merely living for the crown. I want a life for myself, as well. A life for our baby."

"Ah yes. A life for our baby." He spoke softly, not wanting to prod the tender feelings radiating from her. He could have argued, of course, pointed out to her that her absence had made more than a difference, that she had kings and queens and dukes and duchesses begging for her return, that she even had the head of intelligence engaged in the effort, but he didn't.

Like in any operation, finesse was required in dissolving illusions.

If she was determined to remain blind to the impact she had on the lives around her, he wasn't going to force the issue. Inevitably, she would come to the realization on her own.

For now, he was content to let the subject fade as they got to the grittier matters at hand.

"I want you and the baby to stay here at Redcliff. Beginning immediately," he said, anticipating and not being disappointed by the surprise that flashed across her face. It was good to be the one throwing *her* for loops again.

"Live with you?" she repeated.

He nodded. "Beginning immediately. You can enjoy a long and luxuriously pampered pregnancy, followed by a harrowing labor you will never completely forget, and then both you and our child can reside here at Redcliff, where we will raise them together."

"You've got it all figured out," she said quietly.

Eyeing her closely, he gave a slow nod. "Only if you agree."

"And if I don't?" she asked.

"I anticipated your agreement."

The bald statement elicited a dry laugh from her. "How do you propose *we* raise our child when there is no *we*?"

Hardness came to his voice. "I will be a part of my child's life, Jenna."

Rather than being intimidated, her voice grew in strength to match his in intensity. "I'm glad to hear it," she said, "I would expect no less. Nevertheless, we are not in any way, shape or form a parental unit, or a unit of any kind for that matter. Therefore, we have to decide how we are going to manage this together." She punctuated her words with one hand while the other rested over their growing child.

"Acknowledging that you've only recently become aware of it, we have had a long and productive track record of working very well together. I don't imagine parenting will be any less demanding than ensuring the security of the royal family. I am confident we have the required skills," he said.

"Did it occur to you that I might not want to stay here that long? Wrecked thought it may be, I have my own life."

"No one is suggesting you don't have a life, Jenna," he said, dismissing her flare of temper as he would a child's fit. "In fact, I believe it was I who suggested the opposite. What we are talking about is a matter of practicality. Here you have all of the resources of Redcliff at your disposal to ensure our child has the safest and healthiest environment to grow up within. As we are both aware of the fact that you are not currently employed and are residing with your parents, I would think it was the obvious best solution, with the smallest impact to your life, to prepare for the birth of our child and raise them in residence here, cared for with the whole world at your fingertips."

Anger lit her eyes with a peppery spark at the same time as it brought color to her cheeks, visible even in the low night light.

"And what was your plan for the two of us, in all of your wisdom?"

He shrugged, hedging. "I assumed we would have our hands full with parenting."

"And what happens when you get tired of playing house? Or when you identify your next conquest?"

"This is not a game to me, Jenna," he said, deadly serious. "You are carrying my child and heir."

"So, you plan to give up philandering when you become a father?"

"It had been my plan," he said testily.

Her breath caught at his words, but she stubbornly clung to the point she was trying to make.

"What about me? What happens when I am ready to move on? I told you I wanted a full life, with love and family," she pushed.

Something dark and dangerous moved inside him at the idea of Jenna moving on from him. He did not own her, he knew it logically, but that made her no less his. They were having a child together. That meant something more than romantic pleasure. Fair or not, he would not accept the image of her with another man. Yes, it meant a lifetime of fighting the desire that existed between, that threatened to carry them away with a force equal to the canyon carving the Soleil River he loved, but whatever logic worked in her mind, he was certain that its conclusion matched the picture in his mind: the two of them raising their child together. There was no room in that picture for another man. In fact, the mere idea lit his blood with cold fire.

"I would advise against that," he said.

"You can't just keep us locked away forever," she said softly.

Agitated he sped up, strides lengthening as he replied, "And I don't intend to."

Catching up to him, she said, "What did you intend with all of your grand plans? You have many of them I assume."

He did. He had begun putting details into place as soon as he had learned she was pregnant.

He had not questioned that the child was his. He had a sixth sense for truth, and this situation was no different.

He had not attempted to sway or control her behavior. He respected her…knew she had the integrity to mother his child. Nor had it even crossed his mind to take their child from her. He had simply begun making arrangements for their future.

She should be pleased. Instead, she pushed and resisted him. He liked it so much better when she went along.

Though, perhaps he should be grateful she was pushing back. The consequences, his mild irritation, were nowhere near so transformative as the alternative.

Because this was Jenna, he tried again. "None of this needs to be difficult, Jenna."

"I want to get married someday, Sebastian." The statement was soft and delivered without heat, her voice tender almost, as if she wanted to gentle the fact that she was once again throwing his carefully laid plans all to hell. "I want to have a satisfying career and I want to be a wife and I want our child to grow up in a happy, normal family."

His skin felt hot and itchy at her words, his breath constricted, but he resisted the urge to fidget or rub. She asked for things he could not give her for reasons he would never be able to make her understand. Jenna had grown up with regular people, people who could pursue love without it destroying them. He had not. He knew the damage that the obsessive pursuit of love could inflict on a child. It was not her fault that the same tendency lurked in his own blood, that in his DNA lay the same programming. It wasn't even her fault that she had been the catalyst that triggered and activated the potential of his latent disease. No, she wasn't to blame for tempting him, but it remained his duty to protect them both from disaster. "Absolutely not. Marriage is not an option on the table between us." He would not repeat his father's mistakes, even with a woman like Jenna. The price was too high.

Nodding, she placed a gentling hand on his forearm. "I wasn't asking you, Sebastian. I know we didn't plan this, but before it happened, I had always planned to marry and have a family. I still want that."

"You've gotten what you wanted then. You have your very own family now."

"What you're offering is not the same thing, Sebastian."

"The only difference is a piece of paper, Jenna."

She shook her head. "If you think that, I feel bad for you."

With a strange growing sense of dread rising, reaching up to slowly grip and squeeze him around the throat, his voice was more clipped than he intended when he said, "A legal document does not make a stable family, Jenna, and you're a fool if you think so."

"You're right, and that's not why I want it. I want what the paper represents. I want that confidence for my child. I want them to grow up secure in the knowledge that the people who love them will be there for them, a steady, unshakeable unit, bound together by love, commitment and a proudly public promise. I want them to know that no matter what they choose or decide in their lives, they will at least always have a loving family to come home to that is proud of them, even if they make a mistake. I want them to see passion and fire and purpose and to know that they don't have to choose between those things and their dreams and that anything that asks them to, be it person or situation, it isn't right for them." A look of surprise came to her face, as if she had only just heard her words by saying them out loud. "I want what my parents gave me," she added softly, "even if all it does is blow up in their faces."

Love and family. She wanted love and marriage and a happy family. Of course, she did.

He could not offer her that. But what he had to give her was just as good, if she would see it that way. "No other man will care for you as thoroughly as I would, Jenna. You have to sense that's true."

"That might be true, but it's not the same thing. Whatever this strange obsessive thing between us is, it isn't the same thing that carries couples through the highs and lows of a lifetime together, through the difficulties and triumphs of parenthood, or the inevitable desert-like stretches of distance and resentment. I want the thing that does that, Sebastian. I want a fully realized life, Sebastian, not a career and a business partner I raise kids with. I want what my parents have."

"You don't want what they have. If you did, you would have never gone away to chase your dreams in the big city. I read your academy admissions essay, Jenna. I'll buy that you want wholesome and secure, and I can give you at least a version of both, but we both know that's not all you want. You want fast and world-changing, too."

Again, her hand fluttered to her belly, but

she remained serious. "I wanted those things, Sebastian, and look where it got me. Pregnant, alone and no closer to fitting into the world than I ever was—further from it now, in fact. I have to think about what's best for our child. I have to think about what happens when someone better comes along for you. What happens to me when you find a woman you *do* want to marry?" She spoke with her hands, gesturing between the two of them as they walked.

She wounded him though she didn't know it, couldn't know that the intensity of his need for her was so immense that he had not even seen another woman since laying eyes on her. She said she was invisible when it was she who had made every other woman on the planet disappear.

"I can assure you, that won't happen. If I will not marry you, what makes you think I would marry anyone else?" he asked.

"It's too late for silly fears and games, Sebastian. You're going to be a father," she said.

And it was too late for him to stop this train, however much she might deserve the answers she wanted.

He would give her the truth.

"I will not marry you, Jenna."

"Wh—?" she stuttered for a moment as if his bald statement had gone through her chest, before pulling whatever question she had been about to ask back before it escaped. Then she caught her breath, balled up her fist and released it. "I know. That's exactly why we're having this conversation. We need to talk about the future. For our child."

He gave her credit. The words had come out even if her voice had a faint tremor.

"Marriage no longer makes a difference as to whether or not our child will inherit Redcliff, in case that addresses your concerns."

Jenna gasped. "Do not insult me. Wealth is the furthest thing from my mind and you know it." When she wagged her finger at him while she spoke, it gave him a window into her childhood—and one into what a future with her might be like.

But marriage was not required for that future.

"Marriage is not on the table. A stable future with the father of your child, however, is."

"And if that's not enough?" she demanded, stubborn and strong and gorgeous, a knight without armor, defending honor and goodness.

But if honor and goodness thought they could take away what had rapidly become the most important part of his life, he would destroy them both.

"Think about the baby, Jenna."

The words worked like a charm. The righteousness went out of her, leaving exhausted resignation to sweep over her.

Seeing clearly now, she turned to him, stopping them both in their tracks. Her gaze was like a high beam in the night making him certain she saw exactly what he was doing but had lost the will to do anything about it.

"Does it always have to be your way, Sebastian?" she asked.

He held back the wince that wanted to be let free. Whatever she had seen of him, it had revealed too much.

He said, "It's better this way."

Her lips pressed into a firm line while her eyes darted around his face as if she looked for the key to unlocking him. Finally, she asked quietly, "Better for who?" before stepping back from him and continuing along the path.

Her dress, where it showed from beneath the long jacket she wore, was as dark as a blood blot test.

Catching up to her in a matter of strides, he could see the wheels of her mind turning.

"Better for you," he answered. "Our baby. Me," he added.

Her face said he'd surprised her with the admission but she had lost none of her leeriness with him. "Why?" she asked.

"I won't have to worry about you as much."

"If the king can manage, you can, too."

"The king had no choice in getting married."

"This is a *choice* thing?" she asked, incredulously.

"Yes, Jenna. I *choose* not to get married."

"Why?" she demanded, volume rising.

"Because of you, Jenna. It is clearly enough of a challenge to resist our attraction when we are merely colleagues, but I am willing to face the risk for the sake of our child. This is not simply a fear of commitment, Jenna. It is a choice between being a functioning human being and a slavering mess waiting to jump at your beck and call. I choose to provide a better example for our child than that. I'm not not choosing you, Jenna. I'm choosing to be a man, rather than a puppet and a fool."

She was unmoved by the eloquence of his dilemma.

Placing her hands on her hips, she said, "Well, I am *choosing* not to consign myself to a life as your live-in nanny and nursemaid."

With an exasperated oath, he swore, "I will not lead my family down the same path of folly as my parents. What lives between us, the thing that neither of us can seem to deny or resist, is dangerous. It's a cancer preying on our child's future. We both excel in our chosen fields and have experience navigating complicated and delicate situations with tact. We will come together on the matter of our child's future."

At his side, she nodded, uncowed by his low

outburst. "I agree. We will. But not like this. We'll do it like normal people in our situation. I will accept your offer to stay here through my pregnancy and the birth of our child. Once I have a new job, the baby and I will move into our own residence, and the two of us will share custody."

Nothing about the dismal vision she presented aligned with his plans, but why would it? This was Jenna he was dealing with.

Irritation growing into something larger as she pulled away from the future he wanted, he rasped out, "It's too late for that."

They had gone too far.

Again, she stopped, turning to him, her face compassionate. "It's not. We have to be adults about this." She smiled softly, the expression, he assumed, supposed to be comforting. "But it isn't too late to get to know each other."

"It's too late to go back, Jenna," he said. "I've already been inside you. I know that's not enough commitment for you, but it changed everything. As to *knowing* each other…? If you don't know me by now then it's best you not find out exactly what kind of creature you've already invited in."

Her lips parted, breath halted. The tip of her tongue darted out to moisten them and her cheeks flushed, not with fear, but heat. She felt what he felt, whether she acknowledged it or not.

"I already know," she said, hushed as she stared at him, her eyes bursting with the want of him.

He couldn't risk answering her unspoken invitation, so instead he snarled, "You only think you do." And then he turned around to stride back to Redcliff, leaving her to stroll on or follow after him if she liked. He had exhausted his interest in persuading her.

CHAPTER TEN

JENNA WAS AWOKEN in the morning not by unfiltered daylight streaming in through the massive windows of the room Sebastian had given her, as she had expected, but instead by the powerful urge to use the restroom.

Stumbling in that direction she observed that this was because sometime while she had been sleeping, light-blocking screens had descended to cover the windows.

Whether it had been Sebastian's doing or merely something automatic, she didn't know. After he'd stormed off in a fit like that, she wasn't feeling particularly inclined to give him the benefit of the doubt.

Even after stepping into the bathroom that still shook her. Groggy, irritated and filled with memories of her openness beating against Sebastian's closed-off mindset she might be, but she really loved this bathroom.

Washing her hands, the reflection of the tub in the mirror was a siren call, luring her to come and stay awhile, to submerge herself in water and let its wholesome warmth fill her system, working its way into the kinks and knots of her muscles, creating space for relaxation in the way nothing else could.

She had always loved baths, was a true believer in the power of a soak to provide both soothing and profound relief to most of one's physical and emotional woes. But, as if God was truly testing her, even that simple pleasure was denied to her.

Her doctor had advised against long soaks in hot water—it was apparently not good for the developing being in her womb. She was welcome to take lukewarm baths, they'd said, just nothing that might cook the baby.

Motherhood, it seemed, demanded sacrifices long before you had the reward of an actual child.

Of course, it did. And like everything else in her life, she had foolishly rushed headlong into it.

The bath was just another reminder that she'd been impulsive and thoughtless to the point that her body and life were forever and irrevocably changed.

Her stomach rolled and a wave of slick nausea overtook her. Steadying herself on the counter she drew in a deep breath. Standing alone like this, ruminating and mulling and brooding, wasn't good for her. She needed some food in her stomach, and she needed—she searched herself, scanning for any clue inside—action.

Everything had happened so fast and disastrously that she hadn't had time to be present to her body's newfound awareness and tenderness—she had become sensitive to even her own thoughts, it seemed.

But if pregnancy was making her more sensitive, it was at least also making it easier to see her needs.

She had always been a woman to find solace in physical activity. She couldn't get Sebastian to see what he was so obviously and stubbornly blind to, and she couldn't take a hot bath, but she could work out. She remembered the way to his home gym.

Returning to the bedroom, she made a beeline for her bag. In her hasty sweep of her closet at home, she had lost out on bringing along workout gear. But that barrier was easily surpassed by selecting one of the many dresses she'd swept up.

This one was lilac colored and wide cut. It was made from a high-stretch material that flowed with her every move, no motion restricted. It was perfect for a woman who liked to move fast and feel pretty, just like her, because it had been made specifically for her. It was another of her mother's creations.

But her mother didn't make pants.

Because of that, even though Jenna had no problem with pants and had worn them happily for training and while on duty, in truth, she always felt slightly more comfortable in a dress.

But the most wonderful thing about the dresses Jenna's mother made for her was that they'd been made so that she could fight in them. They were always wide and open and made of fabrics that flowed with her movements, rather than getting caught up in her legs.

Her mother knew her and loved her, even if she didn't always understand her.

Jenna would need to carve out and guard a space like that for her baby in the world, with the same fierceness her mother had carved hers.

She hoped she picked up the skillset soon, because after once again letting Sebastian run roughshod over her the night before, she knew she was currently nowhere near doing so.

She wasn't ready to be a mother, to step into the role that her mother had modeled so well—and, despite Sebastian's assurances that they could be a parenting team, she wasn't ready to be a single mother on top of it all.

She didn't know any unwed mothers.

Motherhood was a sacrament to the Priory. One that distinctly *followed* marriage.

A mother was entrusted with guarding,

protecting and nurturing the most precious charge on the planet: another soul.

The fact that she'd been sent home in disgrace the last time she'd been entrusted with the charge of another soul did not bode well for her potential.

Jenna's own mother ran their household and managed the farm books—cooking, cleaning, rearing and administering with grace—while also enjoying multiple painstaking handcrafts, including quilting, knitting, dressmaking, taxidermy and leather tanning.

Everything Jenna's mother did, she did for the express purpose of nurturing her family. Her mother was the center of their family, their source of light and joy, effortless in her work.

But Jenna wasn't ready for that, not really. Yes, she was dutiful and hardworking and had diligently mastered all of the required skills, but until Sebastian, her eyes had been solely trained on bigger prizes and shinier dreams.

They still were, if she were being honest, even if she had tarnished those dreams.

Obviously, there was no way she could go back to her old life now that she was pregnant, she knew that, despite the fact that the queen and Hel and even the king had called multiple times, mortifyingly leaving the message with Jenna's mother that her position was still available to her and that the king had had no right to fire her. But even if Jenna had been sorely tempted to take the queen up on her generosity, it was out of the question now.

Her pride had begun failing on that point, but her pregnancy had come in to shore it up. There was no going back. How would her coworkers ever trust in her again?

The queen remained on the island where the Summer Palace was based, leaving Helene off duty for the time being, free to help transition all of the assets and fortunes of the d'Tierrza family to her new husband's long-lost Andros family name.

Jenna had spoken with Helene one time since leaving the capital—when she'd safely returned from her stolen adventure, and as glad as Jenna was that Helene was back safely, that she had the wonderful and utterly shocking news to share that she'd fallen in love and married, talking to her friend had been like pouring acid in her wounds, reminding her of the depth of all she'd lost and leaving her drained, sad and lonely.

But even if she couldn't return to her old life, even if the specifics of it barely even existed anymore, she could still find a relevant future for herself and child.

Unfortunately, she was also deeply cognizant of the fact that, even with all her skills, training and experience, given her condition, she didn't have many options. She was a professional security woman and her résumé reflected that, but she had a feeling that, regardless of what the law said, potential employers would quickly look over her when they found out she was expecting.

Nobody wanted a pregnant security guard, regardless of whether or not she was fully equipped to do the job.

Well…maybe not *fully* equipped. But she could cope as long as she didn't get the morning shift.

Dr. Milano had assured her, though, that she didn't have much to worry about when it came to the activity level of her chosen profession at her last appointment.

"Should I stop or pull back on my fitness and practice regimen?" she'd asked.

"No," the doctor had said with a sound somewhere between a snort and a cough. "That'd be like quitting training in anticipation of a marathon!" The doctor had laughed again at the last word, as if the idea was true comedy.

If Jenna hadn't known the doctor so well, she might have felt like she was being made fun of.

"I'd heard pregnant women needed to rest," Jenna had said.

Shaking their head, Dr. Milano had said, "Not in general. My advice is to maintain your current level of activity. Your body will tell you when to be delicate with yourself. Otherwise keep fit. You've got one of the biggest workouts of your life ahead of you."

The doctor had laughed again and though Jenna knew the comment was meant in fun, she'd found it mildly irritating, nonetheless.

It was a lot of anticipatory pressure.

As was the endless barrage of decisions she needed to make.

Standing beside the doorway, just before she stepped out into the minefield that was her situation with Sebastian, she let the weight of just how worn-out she was settle over her shoulders, if only for a moment.

It was a bone-deep tiredness that had settled over her the second she'd identified the king's voice in the library and stayed with her ever since—through packing, through the drive home, that first night back in her old bedroom, through the doctor's visit when she'd learned she was pregnant alone—and there was no sign of rest in sight.

Not if she was going to become a mother.

There would be a birth—the biggest workout of her life, apparently—and then an entire new human to care for, a new livelihood to find and maintain, and all of it on her shoulders alone, because despite his words about commitment, the plain fact was that Sebastian had stormed away when things had not gone his way. She had to assume he might do so again in the future.

Far away from the d'Tierrza library, outside the capital and the wealth and the speed, no powerful attraction or flowery internal voice could convince her that she had any kind of future with Sebastian.

He was a duke—stupidly handsome—and one of the wealthiest and most dangerous men in the nation.

Men like him didn't end up with Priory girls, and besides, he'd already made it abundantly clear that marriage was not on the table between them.

Priory girls married nice men who enjoyed children and got softer with age.

Jenna couldn't even picture Sebastian in the same room as a child.

She could not recall ever seeing him occupy the same space as one. Not once, in all her time in the capital.

And as far as softening went, well, age would only make him tougher and leaner. With age, he would dry and tighten, his senses growing keener, his skin thinner, his patience lessening.

He was certainly not the kind of grandfather to play hobbyhorse and sneak treats.

Though, that wasn't entirely true.

She could picture him sneaking candy to his grandchildren—with deadly efficiency and outrageous intrigue, in fact.

He would love it, and so would they.

But where did she fit into that picture?

She didn't know the answer, just like she didn't know what to do for herself or about Sebastian or anything else, for that matter, and dammit, she wanted to take a bath.

But a vigorous workout would be a close second, she told herself, not believing it for a second.

When she didn't encounter him in the kitchen through the time it took her to prepare a light, stomach-soothing breakfast of biscuits, lemon ginger tea and cucumber spears, Jenna assumed she would not be encountering Sebastian today.

Still sulking, she thought with only mild spite as she put her dishes away. They had prodded too close to things he wanted kept private and she had not fallen in line like a good soldier last night, but he could go ahead and sulk for all she cared. She would not be manipulated by what was so obviously a tantrum.

Therefore, she was surprised when she found him in the workout room.

He froze upon her entry, his body deceptively still as he held himself midrep on the seated press machine, the muscles of his upper arms flexed and hard, his thighs planted and still engaged though the focus was on his upper body. As always, the man had gorgeous form.

"Sorry. I'll come back later," she said, mouth

oddly dry for having just finished her tea. And how was it that he managed to look so good, even as she was less than impressed with him?

At her words, he sat forward, shaking his head. "No. Don't let me chase you out."

"It's fine, really," she said. She was quite familiar with being chased out.

"No. It's not. I want you to be comfortable here. With me."

A part of her wanted to laugh at the idea. *Frustrated, attracted, confounded*…there were a lot of words that described how she felt about Sebastian, but *comfortable* was not one of them.

Unfair, the romantic voice inside her chimed in with, and she was startled by it. It had been conspicuously absent since she'd learned about her pregnancy. *You're always comfortable with Sebastian*, it insisted, and again to her surprise, in reviewing her encounters with him, she couldn't deny it. She was always comfortable with Sebastian, even in the most shocking situations. She might also be impassioned and baffled as well, but she was always comfortable.

She'd proven that the line between comfort and settling was a very thin one for her, though. She had to remember it for both her sake and their child's.

"No, really. It's fine. I'll come back later." His presence, even after the way he'd left her on the path the night before, was too distracting to work out anyway.

"I'm sorry, Jenna. I shouldn't have left you like that last night. I—" He stopped himself from completing whatever thought he had been close to sharing. "It doesn't matter. I'm sorry. It was unacceptable and it was my responsibility. You don't have to run away from me." His gaze was clear and direct, respectful and open for her to assess the truth of what he said.

She didn't want the words to begin to work and untangle the knot of irritation and frustration she felt toward him, but like magic, they did.

"It's okay. I'm sure it won't be the last time emotions get high. Thank you for apologizing," she said.

He made a noise in the back of his throat. "Before I met you, Jenna, I might have disagreed. Now, I'm sure you're right. Our child can only benefit for having such a wise mother."

Jenna smiled, though the statement didn't bolster her. The verdict was still far out as to what kind of mother she would be. Letting out a little laugh, she said, "Not my wisdom. My mother's. More than once I've seen her comfort the new mothers of our community, saying, 'When children are involved, you'd better have tissues.' I'd say children are smack-dab right in the center of what we've got going on."

He nodded, green eyes measuring her.

"Among other things." Rising to his feet, he walked to where she still stood near the entrance of the room. "I can't be your husband, Jenna. But I am committing to raising our child with you."

It was, at least, a start. With resignation, she smiled. "I appreciate that. I know a lot of men in your situation would not take that position. We'll figure the rest out as it comes. But really, get back to your workout. There's nothing so urgent you need to stop on my account."

Staring at her for a beat, he said, "You were coming here to use the space."

She nodded. "I was, but I'm good at waiting my turn." She turned, knowing he would continue to insist she remain there if she didn't take the steps to actually leave.

"Before you go, Jenna," he called from behind her.

Turning, she asked, "What?"

"Is it safe?" he asked.

"What?"

"Working out. For the baby?"

If she had not detected a thread of vulnerability in the question, she might have poked fun at him. "More than. The doctor made it loud and clear."

He nodded, and she smiled, touched that he'd cared. The child she carried was his of course, he should care, but it was nice to be included within his net of concern.

She turned once more, again on her way out when he called, "Jenna."

Again, she stopped and looked back at him, "What?"

His eyes had a mischievous look in them that was less sexual than his intense gazes but no less wicked. "Were you planning on working out in a dress?"

Eyes narrowing slightly, she said, "I was."

"Seems rather restrictive," he observed.

Lifting an eyebrow, she crossed her arms in front of her chest, aware that she no longer spoke for herself, but femme folk everywhere in the ageless battle of the sexes. "You'd be surprised."

"By how your impractical fashion choices could facilitate your abduction? No. That's, in fact, exactly what I'm pointing out." He delivered his speech looking down his nose with his head tilted to an arrogant degree.

Jenna scoffed. "Anyone who tried would be in for a rude surprise."

"You deny your attire puts you at a disadvantage then?" he pressed.

She met him head-on, a thrill rising in her blood. "I do."

"I challenge you to a sparring match then."

Her mouth dropped open and a look of impish delight lit his eyes—a look she was well versed in, having witnessed it often in the faces of each of her brothers growing up. He thought he could beat her, and he thought he could prove a point, and because of it, she was honor-bound to prove him wrong.

Her skin flushed at the thought, reminding her that, for all the momentary similarities, he was not one of her brothers. He was a man she had trouble keeping an appropriate distance from under the best, and honestly, most restrictive circumstances.

Wrestling was out of the question.

Even if the thought of it, the idea of moving her body the way it loved to move rather than doing a circuit of repetitions on machines, made both her blood and heart sing.

She shook her head and forced a light laugh, "Not this time."

"Jenna Noelle Moustafa," he said, in a perfect imitation of every playground bully that had ever existed, raising her hackles in the process. "You're scared."

Holding firm, she said, "I am not. I'm mature. And I never told you my middle name."

He shrugged, falling back slightly into a light defensive stance. "I know everything."

"Not quite everything," she said, and then she attacked, faking him out with a feint to the left before sliding right to slip inside her protective barrier. "For example, you don't know what my favorite color is."

And then she danced away, out of his reach and around the nearest machine.

Her pursued her unhurriedly, jade eyes never losing her though she continued to maneuver and weave through the equipment, making her way to the area of open mat in front of the room's requisite floor-to-ceiling windows. Here, at least, she could make out the faint trace of mesh barrier in the glass.

She wouldn't have to worry about throwing him through.

He met her on the mat and they circled one another, eyes locked, their bodies once again transported to a world of their own. The question was: What was he willing to commit?

He knew her on paper, her stats and biography. He did not know her favorite color. The question was now: Would he want to? He said he did, but so far, she had seen him push his own agenda.

Did he care to know something that trivial about her, for the sake of knowing her, the future mother of his child, or did he only care that she was qualified for the position?

Shaking his head, voice bemused as if the fact he faced off with her and the fact that she confounded him were both novelties, he said, "I don't."

"It's pink," she said, the word light and airy, as gossamer-thin as the feelings that hovered in the shadows of her heart while the bulk of her attention tuned to the opening she knew would come. "Well, rose, really," she amended.

She couldn't read the emotion that flashed across his eyes when he said, "I would never have guessed," but he wasn't mocking her. She could see he meant it, but she had no idea if the fact was good or bad to him and not sure if she truly cared.

He'd given her the opening she'd been waiting for. Ducking to go low, small quick steps carried her in on his left.

Rather than try anything dramatic, she merely placed her two fingers against his rib cage before retreating backward, darting and twisting out of his reach as he tried to grab the flowing fabric of her dress.

At a safe distance, as if they were not eyeing each other during mock combat, she said casually, "You've already told me your favorite color, so I get to ask you something different." Bouncing back and forth from one foot to the other, she finally asked, "What's your middle name?" She kept the pressure of her question light, even as it was personal and pointed. Again, she was testing him. How much of himself was he willing to give her?

He answered without hesitation. "Reynard."

"Oh!" she brought a hand to her mouth, letting down her guard with a little gasp. "That's adorable!" She was surprised. The name was sweet and sophisticated, more whimsical and aspirational than she would have imagined coming from the image she had of his parents.

"I wouldn't know," he said, tersely, before jabbing into the opening she'd left, his hand reaching out to her.

Moving with less control than she'd have liked, she was still quick enough to evade him, laughing as she said, "It suits you. Your turn."

"My turn for what?" he asked.

"To ask a question," she answered.

She realized as she moved, her body engaged and enlivened, that she was fully into their game, her mind and heart having left the ominous weight of the previous night behind them.

Sebastian remained quiet for a beat longer, breathing and shifting his weight as he thought of his question, and Jenna wondered if maybe it felt unnatural for him to try to think of a question to get to know someone on a personal level. He was used to analyzing everyone around him, but how many people did he really know?

The thought brought a strange pinching sensation to her chest, one that felt surprisingly like empathy. Was it possible that for all he knew and manipulated about the world around him, he didn't understand the deeper emotional connections that propelled it?

He dispelled her urge to dwell on the tragedy

of his backstory, however, with his next question. "How many times have you thought about my body since the library?"

She felt color come to her cheeks again. The flirtation was unexpected after he'd revealed that he thought that what existed between them was dangerous, but rather than dance away, she engaged with him.

"It's not your body I've been thinking about," she said, voice unintentionally thickening with the truth of it as she spoke. He stopped circling and she flashed him a brilliant smile, a reckless sense of freedom pulsing in her veins.

If he'd thought to get the upper hand with suggestive language, he'd been thoroughly put in his place by her bold response—exactly as she'd planned.

He had tried to use words to glamour her into letting her guard down, but instead, she had turned the tables and thrown him for a loop. She danced into his space again, moving with precision, her person momentarily in the flow zone, stepped a leg behind his, gripped his pant leg and rolled both of their bodies onto the ground.

To her, the entire series of movements had been as gentle as swaying in a hammock. For him, a sudden loss of balance followed by a crash.

Because she had been prepared for the change in their positions when he hadn't, she could turn the momentum of their weight and their fall against him to flip him over once more until she sat atop him.

Then she cocked her arm back, curled her hand into an iron fist and hammered it straight to the space one centimeter from his nose.

"I win." She grinned down into his surprised face before rising to her feet, flashing him a salute, and leaving him in the gym just to prove that he didn't always get to be the one to have the last word.

Later that evening, they made dinner—a mild chicken alfredo liberal with cheeses she'd only ever eyeballed before at the market counter— and ate together casually, sitting side by side at the kitchen island watching the sunlight disappear from the river canyon, leaving a trail of watercolor hues in pink, orange, purple and teal.

They had just finished exchanging stories of their worst professional mistakes and disasters when, reaching for their glasses of water at the same time, the backs of their hands brushed.

Clearing her throat lightly, Jenna said laughingly, "While I will never agree with your absurd idea that falling in love is some kind of calamity, I absolutely concur that it's important we keep our relationship nonphysical. Regardless of whatever else happens going forward, we don't want our relationship to leave our child confused and uncomfortable."

Sebastian nodded at the same time as he seemed to take too large a bite, which required some effort to swallow and a sip of wine to chase down.

"And have you spent any more time considering my offer?"

Watching him closely, she asked, "Which part?" Knowing him, as she was slowly beginning to, the more time she spent with him, she knew there had to be a reason why he was so adamant they live together to raise their child.

"Living here at Redcliff."

It felt cruel to tell him the truth, but she wouldn't lie to him. "No. I just don't think that's a realistic idea, Sebastian. Parenthood shouldn't consign one to monastic existence."

He winced, the expression subtle and fleet, flashing across his face in the blink of an eye, but she caught it. When he spoke, his tone was measured and even. "I didn't get the impression that sex was that important to you."

He thought he could nudge her into his way of thinking by using her inexperience and faith against her, but she was savvy enough to not let him.

"You alone know the limits and excess of my interest in sex, Sebastian. That's not in the least what I meant and you know that, too."

He looked away from her, sipping his wine and staring out into the darkening canyon. Then he let out a breath and turned to her. "Again, it seems I owe you an apology. That was uncalled for. I am rather turned off by the idea of living apart from my child, even within the confines of a normal custody arrangement. However, I recognize I am not the only one with skin in this game, as they say."

For a moment, she only stared at him, conscious that the absurd statement was both a genuine apology and an attempt at being humble. Then, doing her best to keep her words neutral, she said, "Well, there's that at least."

He looked at her closely before a smile cracked his serious face. "You're the only one I apologize to, Jenna. Not even the king."

If he'd intended to metaphysically reach into her chest and squeeze her heart, he'd achieved his aim, the words knocking into her, revealing far more than she thought he realized.

Mistaking her quiet for continued pique, he offered, "Come to the library, we'll have dessert."

Did he mean to draw up the ghosts of their past?

She had barely recovered from his casual confession and here he was again throwing off her equilibrium. Heat infused her cheeks.

Awareness lit his eyes, desire adding an edge to the green fire that always glowed there, but when he opened his mouth, he only offered an explanation. "Tea and bonbons in front of the fire. Nothing else."

There was honest intention in his words, the

look in his eyes held firmly in control, no machination behind his invitation. He was committed, she sensed, to charting the course they'd set.

But though she should be relieved, as they rose to put their dishes away and she joined him in making their way to the library, the heaviness in her heart could only be labeled disappointment.

CHAPTER ELEVEN

HE WAS LOSING control of things with Jenna. Sebastian could admit that in the privacy of his own mind as he opened the library door for her.

First, there had been the kiss in the kitchen—a certain slant of light and a reluctant confession were all it seemed were required to break him of his resolve when it came Jenna.

Then, again, in the library, surrounded with the scent of books, which had now become inexorably linked in his mind with the transcendence of having her, her hair gleaming as it had that original afternoon, and staring into her eyes had been all it took.

He had been luckier in the gym, losing just the bout when she'd landed that knockout punch of a smile, and not his integrity.

So why would he risk leading her into the library yet again? Especially when the ease growing between them continued to erode his guard...

But he knew it was because while he knew

he couldn't give her what she wanted, and they didn't dare explore the passion that lived between them, he could at least give her tea and chocolates.

Hampered and tied as he might be, he still had enough control to do that.

But he was not fool enough to believe they could share the love seat.

Guiding her to one of the large armchairs, he indicated that she should sit while he went to the hidden kitchenette to prepare their tea. When it was finished, an array of sweets and treats laid out for her on a small platter, he rejoined her in the sitting area, strategically sitting across from her in the matching armchair.

They could not be lovers. But it was imperative that they become at least something resembling friends. Studying her as she bit into the first delight she'd selected, he reflected that that was a journey he was completely unfamiliar with.

"This is divine, Sebastian. I've never tasted something so delicious. It's like I can pick apart each individual flavor. Vanilla, almond and that oozy, creamy chocolate."

With her eyes closed, her voice full of her sensuous enjoyment, her presence trailed over his nerves like silk. The smooth pleasure of it— the oozy creaminess of *its* tone—only further grated at the shards of his control.

With a pained smile, he said, "I'm glad you like them."

Her glow in the soft lighting was threefold: the luminance of her spirit, the sheen of her glossy hair, and her enjoyment of the sweets.

He watched, transfixed, the same as any wild creature caught and frozen in the headlights.

When she opened her eyes, they were laughing, their dark brown wells lightened to become amber pools bubbling with fun and ease. For this moment, she was not dogged by the *should* and *ought* that drove her and her radiance was enough to illuminate the sky.

Sebastian swallowed. "Would you like to pick out a book?" he asked, aware of how close he was to some kind of precipice, knowing he needed to step back, yet remaining reluctant to do so.

As if his question had only now reminded her that she was in a library, she scanned the room, her eyes landing on the section of new books he'd curated for her. Her delighted smile impossibly grew upon alighting on the titles.

"I've been meaning to pick up this one for ages now," she said, reaching out to run a finger down the crisp spine of one of the paperbacks.

Sebastian shivered as if the touch traveled across his own skin.

Abruptly, he rose to select a title for himself, walking to the section farthest away from her.

It didn't matter where he went, the titles in this room were only those he loved, could reread again at any time, whatever his state of mind. And that was fortunate, because he needed space between himself and Jenna more than a specific story.

Steadying himself with a breath he pulled a book from the shelf in front of him at random. Of course, it would be Jung. *Modern Man in Search of a Soul*. Reading the title, he almost laughed. It fit that his torture would be narrated as such. The cosmos was possessed of dark humor in spades.

Ultimately, a laugh did escape, and with it, some of the tension. He would take being the butt of the universe's joke if it came with putting the situation in a little perspective.

For his child, he could risk navigating the treacherous territory of his desire for Jenna, particularly as it was the only way to come out on the other side as partners—but the effort didn't need to be given the same valiancy as a war campaign.

Returning to the reading area, he found Jenna already immersed in her book, and this too provided an opportunity: it was easier to remain appropriately distanced around her when her energy and focus were directed elsewhere.

For a moment he watched her read, noting the

rate at which she devoured pages as compared to her sporadic reaches for treats or sips of tea.

Jenna read like she did everything else, with her full self.

He settled across from her after pouring himself a cup of coffee. They read that way for a time—long enough that the next time he reached for his cup the coffee inside had gone cold.

Returning it to the coaster, he looked up to find her watching him with a soft smile.

"It was too late for more coffee, anyway," she said quietly.

He didn't know how long she had been watching and the fact made him feel oddly vulnerable. It was too easy to let his guard down around Jenna.

But still he smiled at her. "It's never too late for coffee."

"You'll be up all night."

He shook his head, "By this point, I'd have to mainline caffeine for it to affect me."

"It sounds like you have a problem," she said teasingly.

Taking her in, bathing in her gentle humor, he said, "Among others. You might say I have an addictive personality." And she was the greatest temptation. But it was his problem to manage the temptation. Or face the consequences. "It runs in the family."

After a pause, she said, "Tell me about your

family." The demand was tentative and probing, as if she didn't expect him to oblige but was too curious to risk not asking. Of course, she would be curious. His family history was her child's history, as well.

He could do no less than tell her.

But where to start? How to reveal the sordid truth of his parents' past to her so that she would know the dangers his rules and demands protected her from while assuring her that he would never falter in the same way and bring that chaos into her or their child's life?

Where should he start?

Jenna was as far from his parents as it was possible to be—innocent, open, free from manipulative tendencies—singular, as he'd told her repeatedly. But what if there were limits to even her compassion? A part of him trembled at the possibility of telling her the story of his family and seeing condemnation in her face for the role he'd played.

At the age of ten, three years into his boarding school career with only one visit from his father—his mother hadn't liked the feeling of the large gothic school building in Austria where they had sent him—he had stopped longing for the kind of relationship with his parents that he'd witnessed among his peers.

He accepted that whatever it was that he was lacking—whatever cold wrongness that existed in his heart, as his father had accused, that had led him to betray his mother and suffer his consequential exile without even the slightest urge to shed a tear—was the same thing which had finally stopped him from longing for that. A light came to his schoolmates' parents' eyes, even the coldest, when they landed on their progeny.

He hadn't been able to recall his mother ever looking at him like that.

His father had been no better.

It had taken three years of waking up far away from home without so much as a whisper for him to realize they just didn't care about him, were completely indifferent.

How would Jenna react?

With no real plan, he opened his mouth and said the first words that came to his mind. "My mother was unfaithful to my father."

Jenna froze, the orbs of her large eyes widening and darkening until they matched his black coffee in color if not temperature. Unlike his coffee, her eyes were filled with beckoning warmth. They called to him, jolting through him, energizing him in a way the beverage never could, gently drawing more from him.

With words, she kept it simple. "I'm sorry," she said softly.

He shrugged her words away. She had nothing to do with the old story. "You didn't do anything."

She ignored the brush-off, asking, "Did it tear your family apart?"

He looked away, a sound escaping that tried to be a laugh but didn't quite make it. "No."

"What happened?"

"At first, my father ignored it. When he no longer could, they lived brief, separate lives."

Understanding oozed out of her, free for the taking when he wasn't sure he wanted it.

"And what about you?"

"At first, I was a tool they used to manipulate each other. Eventually, they sent me to boarding school with rare visits home—where I was always alone—until my mother died when I was thirteen. After that it was year-round school until I turned eighteen. Then, my father died, too. University and early adulthood were a bit wild." He would take those hazy and blurred memories over the crystal-clear snapshots from the years before.

Her bleeding heart ached for him. It was as clear as if the organ had been on her sleeve.

Simultaneously soothing and strangling, her compassion reminded him of a wool sweater, itchy and uncomfortable in its warmth, even when he was shivering from the cold.

"That sounds lonely," she said.

Offering a smile that didn't reach his eyes,

he said, "Compared to what you experienced, I imagine it does. But as far as the denizens of the capital go, it's par for the course. That's hardly the worst of it."

"What could be worse?" she asked.

She employed the most sophisticated technique to gather information—she genuinely wanted to know—and like any good mark, he opened up to her. "Before I realized he already knew, had known all along, I tried to tell my father. I was afraid he wouldn't believe me, so I laid out a case. I took pictures, saved messages my mother had exchanged with her lovers. I collected it all and presented it to my father."

"Sebastian, that's terrible," she said.

He let out a dry sound. "Oh, my mother made that very clear afterward."

She frowned, her eyebrows coming together over the bridge of her nose in the way that never seemed to fail in disarming him. "I didn't mean it was terrible that you did it, Sebastian. It's terrible that you felt you had to. And for your father to tell her that the information came from you?" That she was disgusted on his behalf soothed a deep sense of injustice he hadn't realized he'd been carrying.

His father had mishandled the information.

Sebastian nodded. "He told her all of it. He told her that I had cried as I showed him my evidence. He was trying to make her feel bad, but she didn't. Instead, she called me a crybaby sneak and said that it was unnatural that I would do such a thing to my own mother. And then she walked out."

"How old were you?"

"Seven."

"And your father just let her say all of that to you?" Obvious horror spread across Jenna's face.

"Why shouldn't he? He hadn't even stood up for himself with her. Why would he stand up for me? All in the name of love and marriage. She was the only thing he ever wanted. After she'd gone, he looked at me and told me it was my fault for chasing her away with my spying and that we would have to do everything we could to get her to forgive us."

The frown of her eyebrows was so fierce he felt compelled to cross the space to her, to give in to the driving urge to place a soft kiss there. He could lie to himself and tell himself it was because she looked so sad. He would do it to comfort *her*. "It was a long time ago. It's all right," he assured her. "And it's probably about time we said good-night."

In talking to her, he had opened a floodgate, and one that he didn't entirely understand. All he knew was that he was open and exposed and did not know what would happen if they didn't cut this off now.

Eyes intent, she once again searched his face before lifting in her seat to capture his face between her palms and brush a light kiss against his lips before lowering back down and taking his hand. "It's not all right, but thank you for sharing," she said, sounding like maybe the information had been enough to satisfy her for now.

But of course, it hadn't.

"Why didn't they separate? Why did they stay together when it was so clear they did not love each other? It obviously wasn't for your sake."

The wound was old, but he still winced at her bald statement, even as he shook his head. "My father did love my mother, was head over heels for her, even after he knew she'd been chronically unfaithful." He spoke evenly, as if he was sharing the morning news rather than revealing the most painful of his family secrets.

"What?" This she clearly could not understand.

"My mother was beautiful and charming. Half the men in the capital loved her at one time or another. My father just never stopped."

"That's not love, Sebastian. That's something else. Obsession. Lust. Addiction. Something else."

That she could hear his story and still cling to such naive notions was a testament to her will to believe the best. He appreciated that about her.

But even to preserve that sweetness, he would not sugarcoat the most painful lessons of his life.

"Whatever you call it, it made him weak. It sucked the integrity and honor and goodness from him until he was a shriveling husk, willing to sacrifice and abandon his son. My children will have better." Even for Jenna, he would not repeat the mistakes of his parents. He would break the cycle of visiting the sins of fathers upon their sons.

"What they had was a sickness, Sebastian, and I am so sorry it swallowed you up with them, but it wasn't love. And it isn't the same thing as what we have between us."

It was a wonder she had been able to maintain the level of optimism she had while rising through the national security ranks.

"Do you know that for sure, Jenna? I certainly don't. Before you, my personal code might have been shadowed, but I had never crossed it. Now? I've lost count. And before me, you were living the life of your dreams."

The noise she made in the back of her throat was surprisingly cynical. "Hardly. I was a ghost in the life of my dreams, Sebastian. Just like with your parents, it's not enough. It's not the same thing."

He had to admire the tenacity of her will to cheer him.

"Everyone knew but him. It was mortifying to hear them talk about him. About my mother. That he was a fool and she was a slut was at one time the most popular topic in the capital. In fact, I learned that word overhearing gossip about her."

He'd heard it over and over again, with even greater frequency than the times he had overheard the whispers and snickers about his idiot father—the only one who didn't know about his mother's infidelity. But, of course, like everyone else, he *had* known.

"Oh, Sebastian."

It was incredible the amount of compassion, understanding, and balmy, soothing sympathy she could pack into the single word of his name.

After his childish intervention attempt had backfired, Sebastian's father had consoled himself with booze and gambling until death.

"I survived," he said, shrugging her softness away. "In fact, I thrived. I tore down the old house, and I made an incredibly successful profession out of having all the information and never playing the fool. In a way, you could say I am grateful. The lessons they taught me will ensure our children never have to experience the same thing."

Even if that meant a lifetime of wrestling

with the dragon that was his desire for Jenna. Even if it meant asking the same sacrifice of her. He had to. He hoped she understood now, in a way that she hadn't before, why it had to be this way.

CHAPTER TWELVE

PRACTICAL JENNA, THE GIRL who had always loved to run and jump with her siblings far more than plan imaginary weddings with her cousins, stared up at Sebastian where he stood over her chair, her mind filled with marriage and parents and everything else they'd discussed.

Inside, she wrestled to put his revelations together with his reasons for why things had to be the way they were between them, and also her own wants and needs.

Was it time to accept that certain dreams had already become impossible? That, as Sebastian had said, because they had been together and were now tied for life, she needed to set aside the full picture of her dreams?

While she had never doubted that consequences could be irrevocable, perhaps she had also never truly respected her circumstances as such.

He would not give her the life she'd envisioned for herself, but given what he'd revealed, she suspected that had more to do with old childhood wounds than her worth in his eyes or a playboy's fear of commitment.

Perhaps it was enough, then, that he had promised to care for her and her child.

She would go back to work eventually, of course, but it was no small thing that he had offered to support her and their child. Security, even without love and passion, was more than many women in her situation could hope for.

Their arrangement would not be in keeping with the Priory tradition, but he was right that she had become comfortable breaking with tradition long before she'd met Sebastian.

And though their parents would not be a unit, it was clear that her child would not lack for love from either of them, even if Sebastian had not used the word.

That he felt it was clear in his actions.

He had swooped in and addressed all of the greatest concerns that had been dogging her, outside of nausea and hormones, out of that love. It seemed he would swoop in and take care of her whole life if she let him. If she was willing to agree to his terms.

But was she?

Only if he would meet her halfway. Reaching out, she caught his hand and it was a warm pulsing beacon in her own.

Her mind returned to the imperative desire

that had driven her during their encounter in the d'Tierrza library, more urgent now, more immediate, than it had even been during that first clandestine meeting: she wanted him, and he needed her—to bring him sweetness and light, to temper the darkness of his memories with the offer of a more hopeful future. She was the only one who could do it.

In a world in which she was the preternatural outsider, she had finally found a place made only for her—as long as she was willing to compromise.

Here in the secluded library with him, far from the judgment of even the sun, she realized she was.

Right or wrong, what had been true, from the moment they'd first spoken all the way through until now, was that there really wasn't much she wasn't willing to compromise in order to touch the complicated man before her.

But everyone had their issues, and hers, stark and clear at the end of another long day, which had followed over two months of long, hard days, was that the only place she had ever felt truly at home was in the arms of the man in front of her.

And she was done fighting it.

They'd crossed too many lines, incurred too many irreversible consequences. The only thing left to do was lean in and accept the fall.

If she was going to fall, though, she was taking him with her.

"Take me to your room, Sebastian," she said.

He fought it. In his eyes played out a fierce battle against the nameless force that drew them to each other, as desperate as if his very life depending on it.

The air thickened around them, turning as full and pregnant as she was, until on a frustrated oath, his long fingers came down to curve around her arms and pull her to her feet.

And then he was drawing her through the blur of hallways.

They stopped in front of a door she had not yet entered.

He turned the knob and her heart leaped to her throat.

Inside, the room was palatial.

Far bigger than any single room in the rest of the house, the main suite at Redcliff lived up to every bit of Sebastian's hedonistic reputation.

The walls were dark slate gray, the paint thick and smooth. White trim and accents ensured the deep hue didn't turn the space into a dark cave.

Thick, soft lambskin rugs covered much of the honey-colored hardwood floors, an invitation to play a glossy, luxurious and very adult game of The Floor is Lava.

The centerpiece of the room was a massive bed, its freestanding four-post frame both elegant and minimal. Tall and square, it was made from butter-smooth iron, its lines crisp, clean and almost Puritan for all that it shouted the erotic intended purpose of the room.

The bedding was all ivory, with a thickly stuffed down comforter and a battalion of plush pillows. At the base of the bed, a slash of inky black—a glossy throw blanket lying there like an indolent velvet panther.

Abstract art graced the walls, innocent and sinuous inkblots and lush swirling lines suggesting bodies entwined, snapshots of pleasure and breathless gasps.

There was no doubt the room was built for sex, and at the same time, it could have graced the cover of a magazine.

It was a room like Sebastian.

A charming black-and-white-tiled kitchenette adjoined the room, as if activities here might lead to a need to refuel so desperate that the walk to the kitchen could not be managed.

Other doors led to mysterious places, but her interest in the room faded as her survey led her back to Sebastian, the source of it all.

His green eyes glowed, drinking in her reaction to yet another thing he'd made.

"It's gorgeous," she breathed.

His eyes lit, unmoving from her. "It certainly is."

The soft, warm lighting of the room made her simple lilac dress look elegant.

She didn't care.

She shrugged it off impatiently before undoing her braid, her eyes on Sebastian the whole time. When she wore nothing but panties, she nodded, and the movement sent a ripple through the cool hair falling against her back.

The muscles of his jaw tensed, his eyes burning a swath across her body, and she felt like the most beautiful creature in the world.

He crossed to her, still fully clothed in yet another one of his "rich man's impersonation of the ordinary" costumes—this time jeans and a simple soft sweater.

She brought her hands to his shoulders. He put his own hands on her waist, setting off shivers of electric shock where their skin touched.

Without meaning to, he had once again revealed his need and asked for her, and once again she was giving herself up. As before, there was a sense of the inevitable.

Unlike before, however, this time she knew the firestorm she walked into—had already faced its irrevocable consequences.

He was no softer now than he had been. He made no promises, had flatly refused to give the assurances she demanded even as he denied himself.

But he had opened.

There was no room nor time, nor energy left for games of cat and mouse.

They had to join, become partners on one team. Their child demanded it of them.

The words didn't matter. The intent did.

And the intent in his eyes was as clear as it was powerful.

It didn't matter that he was fully clothed—he was naked to her.

He was subject to the needs and fears that drove him, the need for her, vulnerable and hating it, biting at the bit as surely as a wild colt. The fear of what feeding that need might make of him. He had no freer will in the matter than she did.

"Take off your clothes." She didn't know where the commanding voice she spoke in emerged from, low and utterly assured of obedience as it was.

He undressed for her, his form like a Grecian statue in its perfection.

But disrobing was as far as he was willing to go at her direction.

His urge to dominate clawed for release as his gaze raked across her, sending pulses down her spine. His inner beast paced closer and closer to the surface—to what she knew would be her ultimate delight.

They stared at each other for a long moment, energies circling, breathing synchronized.

And then she blinked, and he was upon her,

sweeping her into his arms and carrying her to the bed, eyes locked the whole way.

He laid her in the bed gently, as if she were delicate and not a trained guard raised with four boisterous older brothers.

His body was even more beautiful than she remembered, his colors more alive, his scent more necessary, weaving into her system, comforting and assuring and settling, the chemical elixir her body craved most in its current condition.

After kissing her lips and her jaw, and leaving a trail of kisses down her neck, he worshipped her breasts, his touch intuitively responsive to her incredibly sensitive and tender flesh. His caresses and kisses, licks, and featherlight nips left her breathless, her back arching, legs rising to wrap around his waist and draw him closer, urging gravity along with the force of her desire.

She wanted to be joined with him as powerfully as she wanted to draw the ecstatic agony out—until she could no longer take it and simply exploded in his arms again.

At the rate he was building her, pushing her higher, nearer that exquisite precipice, she knew it wouldn't be long, certainly not as long as she wanted.

She wanted the stretched-out, languorous experience that their passionate rush in the library had lacked.

She wanted to melt and reform and melt again, over and over with him, all night long.

And there was so much she wanted to do to him still, so many places she'd yet to touch and taste and feel. Things she'd heard of in passing, things her peers had quickly stopped discussing whenever she'd come around.

Images of them—graphic, wet, fleshy—flashed through her mind, and alongside the mastery of his hands and mouth, she couldn't resist.

She burst into thousands of pieces, her atoms spraying everywhere, in all directions at once, as she called his name at the top of her lungs.

Beneath her noise, she could feel his growl vibrating across her skin, possessive and feral.

Rising back to whisper in her ear, he tsked, "Jenna, Jenna, Jenna. I never said you could come."

Still not sure if she was any more than the series of throbbing pulses whose hold on her system had only slightly abated, she somehow found the ability to shiver.

She shocked herself further by saying, "I guess you'll just have to do it again," the words flowing from a part of her she was only now becoming acquainted with.

Hands departing her breasts, he rose over her. "I like it when you talk back to me."

Staring up at him, sex and sin incarnate, she could not believe this, even imperfect, was her life.

All of that force, and it was focused on her.

His eyes had the light of the predator in them, lazily trailing up and down her body, wicked delights promised in their depths as they considered the plains and valleys of her figure.

"You still have your panties on," he observed.

Surprised, she glanced down. Sure enough. Off-white and virginal, the forms of daisies woven into the lace.

"Take them off," he said.

It was a command.

She obeyed, breathlessly lifting her hips to slide the garment away.

Once again, he observed her, saying nothing. Her skin heated beneath his examination. Little about her figure had changed as a result of her pregnancy yet.

Just her breasts were fuller, more sensitive at this stage.

"Open your legs."

Another order.

At this one, her skin flamed, but again, she obeyed.

Spread before him, he continued to stare, eyes darkening. His tongue darted out from between his lips to moisten them, and she swallowed.

His face was shadowed—the expression on his face as he took her in that of a starving man staring at a feast.

"I am going to eat you all up, Jenna."

It was a statement, a promise even, and she shuddered in anticipation.

He didn't disappoint. Her hips bucked when his lips pressed against her intimate folds, the moan escaping high and musical. He smiled his devil smile against her—she felt it—and then she was lost to the expert manipulation of his tongue and lips until they were both drowning.

Recalling his erotic censure, she danced on the edge, holding herself back from crashing.

He rewarded her with greater temptation, hand replacing tongue, long fingers gently stroking as he repositioned his body over hers.

She could no more control the moans and whimpers that escaped her than she could resist the need in his eyes. But because he had not told her to, she somehow held herself on the line of oblivion.

When the hot, thick tip of him pressed at her entrance, trailed and teased along its crease before slightly pressing against her opening only to tease her by pulling back again, she whined.

It took her a moment to recognize the plaintive begging sounds as her own.

Above her, Sebastian was strained, his face a blend of pain and pleasure that she couldn't look away from, both of them frozen for the moment by the strength of their passion.

And then he gave them both what they wanted, what they needed more than their next breath of air. He plunged into her, calling her name as he did, and she broke into a thousand pieces, pieces that she knew only he would ever be able to put back together again.

When she coalesced beside him, it came with what could almost be called peace.

The wave they'd been desperate to escape had come for them, and though they had truly settled nothing—only clouded things, in fact—and she did not know what awaited them, there was relief in finally being out to sea.

The darkness of the room did not press on Sebastian, nor was it filled with ominous recriminations, as he would have expected after having so thoroughly and utterly lost control.

Instead, it was an embrace, as intimate as the one in which he held Jenna, whose deep, even breathing told him she was sleeping.

Was this what his parents had felt, each time they'd fallen back into each other after yet another dramatic separation?

As much as the hard voice inside him wanted to insist that the answer was yes, that he needed to self-flagellate in order to atone, he could not believe it was.

He couldn't associate his parents, chaotic and broken as they were, with the feeling of wholeness that surrounded him.

Again, Jenna had proven him wrong.

Even knowing he was only temporarily sated—that it was just a matter of time before he would want her again, and intensely—he knew he was no more likely to emulate his father than he had been before he'd succumbed.

If anything, he felt more committed to the future that he'd mapped out for the three of them. Having Jenna like this, sharing his home—he was absolutely certain this was what was best for their child, to belong to a healthy and complete whole.

Her compassion had led them through his fears. His reason would lead them through hers.

More confident than he had been in a long time that he would be able to persuade her toward accepting his vision for their future, he drifted off to a deep and dreamless sleep, a smile on his lips.

CHAPTER THIRTEEN

BY THE LIGHT of day, Jenna's conscious noted, what had been clear and certain the night before was more muddled and murkier.

Whereas in the library, his heart and soul bared to her, Sebastian's great fears and the wounded boy inside him were so obvious that she could not help but provide comfort and soothe. Upon waking up alone in his bed, however, she didn't know if she had perhaps done more harm than good.

It had certainly felt that way when she'd drowsily reached for him, only to find him gone. Was he even now reconstructing the distance between them—undoing the progress they'd made toward finding ease in each other's company and the capacity to raise a child together without being a couple?

Judging from the way she'd come to full alertness the instant she realized her fingers caressed empty sheets, she feared she knew the answer.

Urgency to find out for sure, to hunt him

down and demand he account for his feelings, the urge now more important than ever, pushed her, but she refused to let it lead.

Instead, she was measured and slow in her movements as she slid out of bed and located her dress on the floor. Shrugging it on, she left the room sedately, careful not to let the door fall closed behind her.

If she walked into a new minefield, she was not going to go in rushed or frazzled.

But it was not a minefield she walked into.

Instead, it was breakfast. A buffet of light options greeted her. Watermelon and berries, toast, egg whites and pineapple—everything fresh and bright—released delicate scents, strong enough to entice, but not so strong as to make her stomach roil.

And Sebastian.

Though she couldn't put her finger on it, something had changed in him since last night. It wasn't his clothes, though those were as fresh and perfectly suited to him as ever. He wore a simple white T-shirt and slimline khaki pants. His feet were bare.

The intimacy of that, the scene not unlike ones she had witnessed between her own parents, broke the frayed threads of her resolve even as they attempted to rebraid themselves.

He smiled upon seeing her, the skin of his face easy in the expression, no longer tight and fighting to rein in and hide the attraction he felt for her.

He looked…happy.

"Good morning, Jenna. I made breakfast." The little boy that had been hiding inside him, the wounded soul she'd glimpsed last night, was on full display and eager to please her.

And it had been absolutely worth it, she realized.

And she would stay with him—even after the baby was born.

Was it even a sacrifice if she had what she wanted for all intents and purposes, if not in name?

A fluttering sensation in her abdomen answered, her stomach flipping and settling, anchored if not as steady as she would have liked.

Their child would have a family, if not a traditional one. Sebastian would shine as a father, and if the only thing she had to sacrifice for all of it to be true was the title and role of wife, she would have gotten off easy.

Finding enough to root in the resolution, enough good to muddle through, she put on a bright smile and said, her voice oddly stretched, "Thanks. It looks wonderful and I'm starving."

CHAPTER FOURTEEN

SEBASTIAN WATCHED JENNA, her dark hair spilling across the pillows, the long olive contours and planes of her body supple and relaxed in sleep.

She breathed slow and deep and her body was angled toward his, her head tucked into the crook of his arm.

Watching her first thing in the morning, he was filled with unprecedented peace. It had become one of his most treasured portions of the day.

"You're staring. I can feel it." She hadn't opened her eyes yet, but there was a smile threaded through the grumble in her voice.

He continued, shameless. "I will never get tired of waking up with you in my bed. No matter how many times I've memorized it."

Things had shifted between them in the time since all of his intentions had fallen apart, and with them, new possibilities opened. He had risked a sliver of vulnerability with her, and the reward had been paradise.

Since then, he had shifted his main office to Redcliff and spent every spare moment with Jenna. Every day, they cooked and ate together, they chatted and read, they exercised and strolled—and every night they fell asleep exhausted and utterly spent.

She had entered her second trimester, and against expectation, her morning sickness had worsened and, in that time, he had become as expert at managing scents and flavors and spice as she had.

And, early and out of the blue, their baby had quickened, dancing around with such frequent enthusiasm within its mother's still toned and tight abdomen that even Sebastian had had the opportunity to catch a flutter.

He could think of no other time period in his life in which he had been happier. And, though they had not discussed the future again, since that night in the library when Jenna had so clearly seen and understood what drove him, he looked forward to the future. Just as he'd wanted, it would be filled with Jenna, his work and his child.

She cracked open a single glorious brown eye, only to immediately squint in the dappled light that the paned skylights let in. Soon, her other eye followed suit.

With alertness came the focus and warmth that the cold, lonely thing inside him couldn't get enough of—all of it flooding in, as if her eyes were two buckets, slowly submerged in an ocean of her heart.

It was a process he could sample every morning and still look forward to at the end of each night.

"Doesn't that steel trap mind of yours have more important things to memorize? Secret codes, launch sequences, priceless national intelligence…"

"Good reasons to keep it fresh on you, wouldn't you say?"

She smiled, blushing, somehow sweet and innocent still despite the fact that by now he'd had his hands all over her in every possible way—and only wanted to put them there over and over again until the end of time.

The wanting would never stop, he realized.

"Did you sleep well?" she asked, echoing the first morning he'd stayed in bed with her. As he had nearly every day since.

Sebastian shook his head. "No. I haven't had a full night's sleep since you've joined me. I'm exhausted."

Jenna chuckled though he only spoke the truth. "You're uncontrollable."

He didn't bother to deny it. Instead he pulled her hand to his lips to softly nibble the tips of her fingers. "And we have so much time until the afternoon…"

Jenna scoffed but made no move to pull her hand away. "Spoken like a decadent city duke."

"I'll accept decadent, but Redcliff is deeper into the country than your own home."

She scoffed. "You were always at the capital."

He shrugged. "There are more women in the capital."

"Right," she said flatly, eyebrows becoming a straight, unamused line across her face. "Well, I'm going back to my room now." She swung her legs over the edge of the bed, at ease and saucy, even absolutely naked.

It stole his breath away.

Until she brought a hand to her stomach and moaned.

Sitting up, recognizing the signs of her nausea, he let himself be guided by the powerfully possessive urge to care for her that had developed within him over the past month or so—since he'd stopped trying to deny it.

Sliding from the bed himself, he found one of his softest T-shirts for her and untangled her panties from the sheets. She muttered a dark thank-you, and he was tempted to smile. But only tempted.

By now he'd learned that his amusement would not be tolerated at the moment.

"Time for breakfast," he said, holding a hand out once they were both dressed.

She took his hand and went with him willingly.

The habit—taking his hand and going with him—was one of his favorite things about her.

Holding back his smile, heedful of the inner knowledge that the morning bear version of Jenna had no interest in his amusement, he walked them back to the kitchen at the heart of the house.

Jenna didn't want words. She wanted relief. And, as ever, he'd hunted the information down until he could provide it.

After tweaking and more research, he'd perfected his morning offering to her, food as remedy, and, like everything he did, he'd been extremely effective. It had become their morning ritual that he prepare it for her first thing once they got to the kitchen, before he even had coffee.

It was a small thing, the least, in fact, that he could do to show appreciation for the physical burden she took on for both of them. It was a way he could show that even though he couldn't give her everything she asked for, he could give her what she needed. He could provide care.

She had shown him something that night in the library. It was not he who had been faulty or unworthy. It was something in his parents.

By so clearly seeing his childhood intentions, with no hint of castigation, she had vindicated and validated his instincts. He *could* see the right course of action, not merely the most expedient. Keeping her safe then, giving her the life that those same instincts had driven him to plan for them, was the least he could do.

He had not been wrong in that, and he was not wrong in this. She wanted their child to have what she had had. He did, too. And so they would, even if not exactly the same construction. They would have a place to grow.

With so much nurturing, it was no wonder Jenna had become the woman she was. In small ways, he'd tried to show her over the past month that he could not only match but surpass her upbringing in terms of attentiveness and care, if not tradition and structure.

She would be a wonderful mother and he would make sure she had every support she needed.

The thought warmed him as they walked— as it always did.

In the kitchen, he set the wilting Jenna at one of the stools tucked under the large kitchen island's thick marble countertop and flicked the switch on the countertop kettle.

She lay her forehead on the marble—no doubt appreciating its smooth coolness in the face of her furnace-like metabolism—and he prepared her tea.

When the tea had finished steeping, he added a half teaspoon of honey to the hot liquid and laid six ginger cookies on a plate. No more, no less. This was the first course. They had a routine.

When three of the cookies were gone and her color steadier, Jenna aimed a much stronger smile at him. "I'm human again."

Leaning in close, he kissed the space below her ear, where her jaw and neck met. "I'm glad to hear it," he said, savoring the shiver of her response.

The catch in her breath.

She drew in a long, slow inhale, her nostrils fanning slightly with its strength. She was smelling him, he realized, and her body sighed closer to his. The attraction between them was only enhanced, magnified by the side effects and superpowers of her pregnancy.

By the time she trembled out her exhale, he was hard as rock and ready to take her at the island.

Her mind was on more mundane subjects.

Voice steadying as she spoke, she said, "Every day, I'm surprised again at how well it works. The internet is full of old wives' tales that only make things worse."

He continued kissing her neck, murmuring, "I do my research and don't leave things to luck."

She chuckled softly, breath turning shallow. "No, I don't suppose you would. I mean, except for contraception," she teased.

Smiling against her skin, he made his words

temptation against her neck. "How am I to know you didn't sabotage and entrap me, Jenna, my sweet? It's very bold of you to highlight my behavioral contradictions. There are leaders of nations who would hesitate to do so."

Again, she shivered against his lips. "Spoken like an espionage mastermind." He could hear the smile in her voice, knew it was there on her face without looking, but also knew the fact took her aback—that she realized that was what he truly was, saw it without illusion, but still chose to lean into him. Each time was a tiny stitch repairing the idea that there was something evil about his thorough nature.

His lips traced her skin, imbuing his words with his wicked intentions. "And yet, you're still here. What does that say about you, Jenna?"

"Only terrible things, I'm sure. In fact, I can't for the life of me think of a reason why I'm even here with a playboy like you." Her voice was saucy and airy, even as it dared him to name a reason.

He closed in on her, enveloping her smaller frame from behind, arms coming to wrap around her middle, taking the weight of her breasts on one forearm while the other hand remained free to play. "What can I do to jog your memory?"

"Hmm…" she murmured, and he could feel the vibration where their skin connected. "I have to think like a mastermind myself if I'm going to take one on. That means information. Give me information." The words were as heavy and thick as her breasts.

He smiled into her skin, inhaled her scent, and mind, and soul. "It's so sexy when you talk dirty."

Always down for a game, a blush rose on her cheeks and wickedness flashed across her eyes. "Tell me—" She stopped, exhaling as his fingers found her nipples. Then, drawing another heavy breath, she continued, "Something that would break you."

He stilled.

The air around them thickened and pulsed in time with his erection, the intensity of its sudden rage and drive for dominance on par with the vulnerability she'd so casually asked of him.

She wanted a secret, a weapon she could use if the moment arose—the dark currency he dealt in on a daily basis, that he knew the power of.

She asked for a bit of the shadow he wore like armor, and she knew it, her brown eyes unflinching and bold in the request.

For compromising, this was the price she asked of him—a stake to drive in his heart. To make himself vulnerable.

So be it.

His hands traveled back down and over her breasts and lower, his fingers dancing along the bare skin of her belly until he reached the top edge of her panties. He slid them down as he pressed closer to give her what she wanted.

"No husband on earth has ever wanted his wife the way I want you. Will never stop wanting you… What's between us, Jenna, goes so far deeper than something as paltry as marriage," he said, positioning himself to enter her from behind at the kitchen island with the watery light of the morning streaming through. Then, lower, softer, he confessed, "I've never cared about anyone or anything as much as I do about you."

"Sebastian." She turned his name into a gasped interjection, sharp and his for the taking right as he placed himself at her entrance.

Outside the sky cracked open, rain pounding down from the clouds against the roof and windows.

But he held back at the gate, their breath suspended, her wet heat searing and teasing him. He had given her the stake. Did he risk now laying himself bare?

He resisted for as long as he could, held the line until there was nothing left of him to grip. And then he worshipped her as they both required.

Thrusting inside her, his erection harder than it had ever been in his life, he gave her his greatest fear: the knowledge that she held the power to hurt him, as deeply as his parents.

She met him with every deep stroke, received him with shuddering moans and gripped him for more in exchange for the power to ruin him.

"Sebastian," she cried again, and he heard the question in the word as much as he felt it in the increasing strength of her body's rhythmic pulses around him.

He had given her what she wanted, and she teetered on the edge. She wanted to fall.

Entirely in her thrall, he could do no less than give her what she wanted.

The orgasm that ripped through was her strongest yet, gripping him in a vice storm unlike any he'd entered in his long, bacchanalian life. So strong she stripped him of his control, tearing him into pieces as she went on, milking him until he was wrung out and dry.

They collapsed against the island together, their heavy breathing suddenly loud in the soft morning light of the kitchen.

She moved first, her palm slowly creeping across the shining marble surface to intertwine her fingers with his and squeeze. And with the gentle pressure, the tight, angry knot in his chest, the little boy who couldn't forgive his father for being a fool, loosened.

Returning her squeeze, he drew in a deep breath as he lifted his weight from her back. She straightened with him, snuggling back against his chest instead. He wished he could have said the move didn't warm him, but lies were a weak man's defense, and while he might have a weakness in Jenna, he was not a weak man.

He wrapped his arms around her and held her close for another moment and breathed her in deep, wanting her only more for the new weapon she held over him.

Straightening, he adjusted her shirt before placing his hands on her hips, holding them with gentle pressure as he eased out of the lock of her body. Her breath hissed out as he did, resisting the movement.

Lodged thick and tight within her as he was, it felt as if higher powers than their bodies protested the breaking of the primal connection.

Moving slowly so that he didn't chafe her as he withdrew was its own oversensitized communion, and he was present for its entirety until all he could feel was cool air all around him.

Watching it as he was, he noticed traces of blood and stilled.

"Jenna," he said, a strange rushing sound in his ears.

"Hmm…?" she replied, turning to look at him.

He lifted his fingers, where faint traces of blood lingered. As an experienced adult male, he was familiar with women's bodies and wasn't squeamish about a bit of blood. As a prospective father, however, he had no sense of the level of danger. Without the requisite knowledge, he was at a loss for what to do, starring at what could be normal or could be disaster, absolutely powerless.

For her part, the color fled Jenna's face, pale panic chasing the pigment away from even her freckles. He had seen that kind of reaction once before in his life, before his mother had passed out after she had witnessed him fall from a tree and sustain a compound fracture as a child.

Sebastian braced Jenna immediately, though he doubted that was what was happening to her.

She was a royal guard. She couldn't faint at the sight of a little blood. He refused to believe it.

Instead, she turned frantic, separated from him to twist and face him. Steadying herself with his arm, her grip clawlike in its ferocity, she gingerly probed herself with her other hand. When her fingers came back laced with blood, too, she said, her voice pitched low with fear, "We have to go to the hospital."

CHAPTER FIFTEEN

SEBASTIAN ASKED NO questions as he drove. Or maybe he did, and she just hadn't heard them.

Either way, when they parked, and he opened her door, she realized the journey from Redcliff to her doctor's office had passed by in a vague blur, the colors seeping and bleeding together, aided in their distortion by the fall of rain.

She was glad it was raining.

Her mother had had a miscarriage. She remembered it.

The very late pregnancy had been an exciting surprise to the whole family.

At six, Jenna had been so excited to pass on the baton of being the baby of the family.

She had already filled two boxes of arts and crafts for the new baby when it had happened.

Her mother had been so sad.

Jenna's doctor had assured her that while miscarriage was relatively common in the first twelve weeks of pregnancy, with the increased morning sickness she'd been experiencing and safely making it past her first trimester without any trouble, she likely didn't have anything to worry about it.

A nurse ushered her into the back, asking Daddy to wait in the lobby while they took Mama's vitals. If they had come by for a routine check-up, Jenna might have had time for the expression on Sebastian's face as he memorized everything around them.

Emotions flashed across his countenance, but she didn't pay attention.

"Here, love, you know the drill." The nurse's voice was soothing, calm and easy as she handed her the sample container as if emergencies like this happened all the time.

In Jenna's line of work, she knew they did.

Just not to her.

She was the one who saved other people from emergencies. She was not the one who had them.

Except now she was the one sitting in a hospital gown on a table in a silent exam room.

Her heart stuttered.

And then Sebastian was there, his presence like a shadow in the room, and something in her felt marginally steadier.

Coming to stand beside her, he took her hand.

The doctor came into the room, stopping her where she was. "Well, Jenna," she said, looking at the chart in her hands, "that entry was nearly as dramatic as when you came into the world bottom-first, but I—"

Dr. Milano, the grandparent-like figure that Jenna had never seen uncomfortable in her entire life, stopped talking upon noticing Sebastian glowering darkly at Jenna's side.

At first, the doctor stared at him in mild wonder. Then she squared her shoulders and gave a glare of her own. "Glad to see this pregnancy isn't some kind of miracle. You never know with a woman like Jenna."

Jenna's mouth dropped open. For good and ill, the staff at the country hospital that Jenna had grown up going to didn't always maintain their professional distance. Only Dr. Milano's breach of etiquette reminded her that this was Sebastian's first time accompanying her to the office, though. He had missed the early appointments while she remained at her parents, and she had not yet transitioned to the more frequent visit schedule of later pregnancy.

For his part, Sebastian's hand tightened around Jenna's, but he sounded easy when he said, "Agreed."

The response wasn't what the doctor had expected and resulted in some wary eyeballing before she finally turned back to Jenna. "We'll do an ultrasound, but it is just us being extra cautious. In my opinion, everything looks well within the realm of normal pregnancy bleeding.

You're still feeling terrible every morning?" the doctor concluded cheerfully with the question.

She nodded. "Like clockwork."

"Excellent," the doctor said. "That's the best sign that everything's still on track. Ready?"

Nodding, Jenna lay back on the table, positioning herself as she had the very first visit. This time, thankfully, she had progressed past the wand. She had become leagues more comfortable with Sebastian in the near month they'd lived together but hadn't quite progressed to wanting him in the room during invasive medical procedures.

Sebastian positioned himself on the opposite side of the bed from the ultrasound machine and doctor, his entire posture thrumming with an intensity that had nothing to do with desire but was no less fierce for it.

The doctor prepared the jelly, warning, "This is going to be cold," before spreading it on Jenna's lower abdomen.

Jenna's heart beat furiously in her chest, a strange pressure mounting. The doctor had said they thought everything was fine, so why did Jenna's sense of warning refuse to wane?

She was at the hospital with the father of her baby for the first time—it made the fact that they would be parents real in a way that all of their talks and time spent together had not.

And then the room filled with the thundering

hoofbeat sound that heralded the beginning of a new era in her life.

Beside her, Sebastian froze, his entire focus halted and held by a sound, stopping him as powerfully as it did her—she felt it all as if experiencing the shock along with him through the special bond they shared.

"There's the little one. Sounds strong and healthy," the doctor said, ear cocked, listening to the sound, moving the wand around, and watching the screen until exclaiming, "Ah. And there we are."

The grainy black and gray and white of the screen showed an obvious head and body. Limbs and bones appeared and disappeared on the screen as the doctor moved the wand around over Jenna's abdomen, happily chattering away while the baby's heartbeat thundered in the background. "Baby looks good, now let's find the placenta, shall we... Ah, yes. Here we go. Attachment is strong, and the cord is nice and thick and not tangled in there."

The doctor's words were comforting, affirming.

Jenna barely registered them.

Her baby was beautiful. It was a blob with bones and a head, yes, but it was a perfectly formed head. Genius bones. And though she knew it was absurd, she could have sworn she saw Sebastian in the shape of its little skull.

Her child was astonishing, instantly the most amazing being she had ever seen in her life.

And seeing that perfection for the first time, hearing the drum of the heartbeat that would be the rhythm of its entire life, Jenna knew that what had been enough in the face of all of Sebastian's trauma, and over the past month—playing house and making love—was by no means enough now.

In fact, *enough* wasn't even the right bar to set.

Magnificent. Spectacular. Abundant.

She and her baby deserved not what they could get, but the very best life could offer. Looking at them, it was suddenly, irrevocably and abundantly clear that they were part of something large and longer, the vast length of human history, and that each and every linked soul in it was a kind of miracle, utterly and absolutely deserving of every specific dream and wish their heart desired—herself included.

She could never accept *enough* for her baby. Her mother could never accept *enough* for her, and so on, unbroken, backward and forward. She could not settle.

And leaving things like this, the future ambiguous in its lack of specific key features she had always wanted it to include, would be settling. For her, for their baby and even for Sebastian—though he still didn't get that he too lost out by denying them what she wanted.

But accepting anything less than exactly what she wanted would be settling. Like sins revealed in the face of God, filled with a new awareness of her baby, she could no longer do it.

In the halogen lights of the doctor's office, in the face of the being whose presence was the manic galloping sound in the room, she realized it was never a matter of *enough* but *how much*—how much life and joy and love she could shove into the precious short time she would have to be her child's world.

Like cosmic curtains had been opened, clarity flooded Jenna. Her baby deserved a whole family. *She* deserved a whole family. And her baby also deserved a rich childhood full of laughter and warmth and pride in family and confidence in place and belonging—a strong starting place from which to jump off from when the time inevitably came for them to leap off and create their own belonging and place in the world.

Just like she had had.

Sebastian had been right when he'd insisted that she belonged in the capital, and in the queen's guard. He'd been trying to tell her, he'd even shown her, but it was only now she was seeing—she belonged wherever she put in the time and effort to be. She belonged in the place she had been building for herself all along. Destiny wouldn't carve a place for her, it merely provided the tools and circumstances with which she could build one for herself. And, as she'd always known but seemed to have recently forgotten, it was up to her to establish its shape and boundaries. It was up to her to identify her moral standard and stick to it. She had to do what was right according to the voice inside. She could not settle. Not even out of love.

With the tsunami of fear for her child broken, the bright light of understanding had dawned, and in it, she was left to see exactly the wreckage she was dealing with, and it was love. Absolute, devastating love. The thing Sebastian had so feared had gone right ahead and snuck up on Jenna, caught her in its net and convinced her to forget her integrity as surely as it had his father.

But she had learned.

She would have to pick up and repair all of the parts of herself that had been willing to accept anything less than the fully realized life experience she wanted for herself and her child—including all of the rubble of the rest of her fears, desires, loneliness and illusion.

She loved Sebastian.

But as much as she wanted him, and loved him, she couldn't have him, not with what he offered.

If it wouldn't mean losing sight of the mesmerizing creature on the screen, she would have squeezed her eyes shut in resistance to the dawning realization.

As it was, it was their child on the screen that gave her the strength and insight to finally make her stand.

The joy of sharing this moment with Sebastian in the flesh, after the threat of danger had passed, was matched only by her dread of knowing she had to walk away from him.

He could not have them if he could not give them the life they needed. His wounds and misconceptions could not be allowed to shape the direction of their lives, no more than her own could.

She would call her friends back and apologize. She would return to her job because it was her passion and calling and she was good at it and loved it.

And she would be a phenomenal mother, just like her own.

"Well, everything looks good to me. I'd say you can head home. No strenuous exercise for a week or so, but as long as you don't have any more bleeding you can probably just get back to life as normal."

Sebastian's voice croaked out, as if rusty, thick and heavy, "Thank you, doctor."

The doctor nodded after another assessing glance. "Glad to meet you."

"Likewise," he said in a voice she'd never heard him use before. She couldn't call it the real him, but it was warm and friendly with genuine happiness.

He was being cordial to the doctor caring for his unborn child.

The doctor stepped out with the admonition to take as long as they needed, and then they were alone in the room.

Without words, Sebastian wrapped his arms around her, enveloping her in warmth that seeped into her pores and tempted her to accept less than she should.

But she had a responsibility to her baby. Sebastian would provide for them while she was on leave and after, ensuring their child would have everything it could ever want or need.

But Jenna didn't need to live with him for that to be true.

And more than that, she no longer could.

It didn't matter that she wanted him exponentially more with each taste she got of him. It didn't matter that he wanted her with equal intensity. It didn't even matter that they seemed to have been *carved out of the same stone*, as Priory tradition waxed poetic.

What mattered was the environment and example she provided for their child.

Mothering was about more than meeting basic needs.

It was about creating a home bursting—overflowing, really—with love. It was about showing through actions how to be a decent person in the world. It was about being present and there for the little things so that you could be trusted with the big. Mothering was about getting in arguments and holding the space to get over them, without the fear that things might fall apart. About showing that people grow and change but that authentic love remains.

It was about what her parents had built for her and what she wanted to build for the developing human she carried.

Mothering wasn't about all-encompassing obsessions and secrets and shame—it didn't have room for things like that.

Mothering was about love.

She loved Sebastian, and wanted his love in return, but whether destiny had ordained it for her or not, she could not accept him with anything less. That would only be bad for everyone involved.

She wanted him to love her enough to respect the vision she had for her future.

"The baby is safe, Jenna."

Sebastian's voice cut through her thoughts, drawing her attention to the long stretch of time that she had gone without speaking.

He thought she was still worried about the baby.

Turning to him, she opened her mouth to correct him. "No. I—" But he didn't let her finish.

Instead, he kissed her, and in it she felt his fear and wonder, as well as an overwhelming wash of possession, of her, yes, but of their baby, as well—all of it as if they were her own emotions.

If there had been any doubt as to his cherishing of her, she had none now. And if there had been cause to question his intentions toward his child, his reaction had obliterated it.

She should have expected it.

Sebastian did not dote on or love anything. He lifted it up on a pedestal and then proceeded to decimate any threat thereto.

It was not the same thing, Jenna knew, but it was Sebastian.

Of course, his child would be treated the same.

The tidal wave of all of the emotional highs and lows of their past month together—mornings and nights, making love as if they were honeymooners, cooking and eating together, relaxing and reading together, the nausea and conversations about the baby and moments just being quiet together—infused their kiss.

It was going to kill her to let go of the only place that had ever naturally felt like it belonged to her.

It felt like kissing him goodbye.

All she could do was ride the wave as it carried her through to its inevitable end. She could not stop the tide.

He pulled back, eyes closed as if he lingered, savoring the taste of her on his lips.

The tears that had threatened throughout the

episode sprung up and made their move now, filling and spilling in heavy, fat drops.

He opened his eyes. Alarm flashed through their mesmerizing emerald depths.

"What's wrong, Jenna?"

"I can't do this, Sebastian." Her voice broke.

His eyes narrowed. "Can't do what?" he asked.

"This. This crazy thing between us. This is no kind of family for a child. We have to stop. I won't live at Redcliff. I told you it's too late for games. I'm not willing to play house. If you don't want a family, I'm going to find a man who does."

He stilled, becoming almost unreal with his lack of motion.

"Unacceptable," he rasped, his voice implacable. Then, he added, the words hushed, "You know how I feel about you."

The vulnerability was a dagger in her heart, but she could not relent. "I haven't blamed you, Sebastian. Not once have I blamed you for the wreck that my life has become since you've come into it. I take responsibility. I went with you willingly, over and over again. That's my fault. But I'm stopping it here, and you're going to let me. You're going to walk out that door and wait for me to call you and you're not going to monitor my calls, and you're not going to have me followed. And you're going to do it because if you don't, it will become your fault, and I *will* blame you, and, for whatever reason, *that, of all things*, matters to you." She had wrung out every word her heart had been holding up its sleeve, including nuggets she hadn't even understood before saying them out loud.

The thing she saw—the bond she felt that defied her sense of herself as a modern woman of the world—he felt it, too.

He felt it and didn't know what to do with it, didn't recognize it for what it was, because he had never felt it before.

Her heart broke for him.

But her child didn't deserve to inherit his wounds.

She didn't deserve less because of them.

And it wasn't her job to save him from himself. If he wanted what she represented, he could do the work.

His dragon eyes glowed, showing her words had hit their mark.

Looking at him, she noticed for the first time that he was completely disheveled—for him.

His hair was tousled, the midlength sandy blond waves lying akimbo as if he had recently run a hand through them. He wore jeans and a crewneck T-shirt, and his face was shadowed with a day and a half's worth of growth. He was the most human looking Jenna had ever seen him.

But she wouldn't break.

"I will never stop wanting you. Why can't that be enough?" His voice was ragged and harsh.

She shook her head. "It's not the same thing."

"Isn't it? I can't say I've seen otherwise."

"I know, Sebastian. And I feel sorry for you. We are the masterminds behind our own lives. You taught me that. But you're so afraid of repeating your parents' mistakes and cruelty that you've consigned yourself to living half a life. You have to be the one to change if you want something more." She didn't imagine people often felt sorry for him, but if he was too much of a fool to see what blossomed so obviously around him, she couldn't help him. She couldn't save him from himself, any more than he could save her.

His expression said as much.

His words were tight, but he managed to squeeze out the words with dry derision. "Don't worry on my account."

Her eyes narrowed at him.

"I wanted you the moment I laid eyes on you, Jenna. I didn't care what walk of life you came from, about your abilities, none of it. That's more than the king can say about the queen. Everyone calls what they have love. Why can't you do the same with this?"

"He loves her, Sebastian," she said, aching for this man who could see through everyone he encountered but could not see what was so obvious to all those around him.

"It's another word for the same thing."

She could not allow him to evade, could not let him slide around her defenses, not without meeting her demands. There was too much at stake. "Love and marriage are about more than physical passion and obsession."

"And so is this," he said, gesturing between the two of them. "I told you that you were singular, Jenna. That wasn't a lie. What is between us is, as well. You think that what exists between us is normal, like it happens like this all the time because it's the only thing you know, but it's not."

"Our child deserves a real family, Sebastian," she said. "I deserve to be loved."

"Loved?" he said darkly. "Sweet Jenna. I drink from you until there is nothing left. I possess you, body and soul, until you can't remember if you ever had a dream before I came into your life. I thought once would be enough. I was wrong, and now I need a constant supply—and you do, too. Love pales in comparison to how I feel about you. You think our child needs a happy family, fine, but don't for a minute lie to yourself about what you want, Jenna. You won't be happy with something as watered down as love when you could have me."

The truth of his words lanced through her,

impaling her, lodging in her chest, pinning her to a lonely future.

Her hand came to her abdomen by habit, reminding her. *Not lonely.* She wouldn't be lonely for a long time.

She would have their child, and her friends, she thought, realizing that something had shifted inside her. She could pick up the phone and call her friends and family at any time. She always could. The knowledge gave her the strength she needed to hold her ground. She loved him, but she wouldn't be a martyr.

"You're wrong. I know you are the only one for me. A part of me has known it from the beginning. You're not the only one who knows things. But life sometimes requires sacrifice, even a once-in-a-lifetime one. Our child is worth that sacrifice."

She was breaking apart inside, but it was okay. For the first time since they'd parted at the d'Tierrza gala, she could feel her inner compass again—could sense the magnetic pull of *truth* in her cracked-open and bleeding chest. "It's all or nothing, Sebastian. I deserve that."

He stepped back from her as if the movement hurt him, his eyes sliding toward the blank screen of the ultrasound monitor that had only recently given them their first image of their child. Then, as if he were a thousand years old, his bones brittle and fragile and rigid, he walked out of the room.

He hadn't spoken, but he had given her his answer.

She watched him go, staring after him, numb for an eternal instant.

When he had been gone long enough that the sounds of the clock ticking and her breathing had become overloud to her ears, she put her face in her hands and cried like she was a baby.

CHAPTER SIXTEEN

SEBASTIAN SAT BEHIND the wheel at a lonely fork in the road.

A right would lead him to the capital, where he could lose himself in work, raking his mind through the muck in order to forget what kind of man he was.

A left would take him to Redcliff, the house that he had spent the past month transforming into a home with Jenna.

His mother had hated Redcliff—she had thought it too far away from the city, too high in the mountains, and too rainy and foggy. She had called it moldy.

Jenna was nothing like his mother, but for one similarity—her uncanny ability to bring a Redcliff man to his knees.

Sebastian had sworn he wouldn't be like his father, that his weakness would not live on beyond him.

He had come so close to keeping his word.

And then he had encountered Jenna.

Jenna's face, aching as he left the hospital room, was seared into the backs of his eyelids, taunting him every time he closed his eyes.

He knew he was a cold man, but here he was, at a new level, abandoning the mother of his child after she'd put her heart on the line.

The immensity of impending fatherhood swept over him once again, washing over him with a sense of vertigo more concrete than ever before, now that he had seen and heard his child.

A right was his life in the capital, unchanged, pretending to be the city's most notorious playboy, all the while immersed in the work of maintaining the international security of the country.

A left, a family life.

Fatherhood, watching his child grow, evening walks and morning after morning with Jenna.

But that was wrong.

A left wouldn't bring him any closer to a future with Jenna. If it could be so simple, he'd have already made the turn. Only giving her everything she wanted from him would bring him closer to a future with Jenna. Only letting go of his inner demons was good enough for her.

He had fought and striven to be a man far re-moved from his parents his entire life, and in rigidly controlling his life, in ruthlessly filter-ing what emotions he allowed in and out, he had merely repeated their mistakes.

He had made himself into the impossible-to-love creature that he'd always feared he was, and now that creature was hell-bent on bringing the same fracture to his own burgeoning fam-ily. And it was all because he couldn't deal with his own feelings and fears—his obligations—like an adult.

The choice was clear when he thought of it that way. There was no choice.

Tearing himself open and letting her shed light into the deepest corner of his shadow was the only option. Facing his fears to give her what she wanted, over and over again—endlessly—was the only way.

Jenna was the mother of his child, identified by a plan and process he'd had no role in, but that had somehow led him to the right woman. She had loved even with the barriers he had put up to stop it from happening.

His body and what scarred bits remained of his soul had recognized her, and his need for her, long before the strategic mind that he was so proud of had.

In much the same way, his heart now dragged the same resistant mind toward acknowledgment of what his instincts had known immediately: he was in love with her.

It didn't matter if they were married or not, she already had the power to make a fool of him, as his mother had his father.

He was clearly a fool, driving away like an ass instead of standing beside her.

Beside the mother of his child...and the woman he loved.

The admission slammed into him like a wrecking ball, demolishing the last protective wall that stood between him and the truth.

He loved Jenna.

Utterly and absolutely. He had from the moment he'd laid eyes on her, and so he had also been right.

Because he was a man who had no qualms and much means when it came to protecting and pleasing that which he loved, she was the most dangerous woman in the world.

And the only defense the world had against her was the fact that she was alive with an inextinguishable inner goodness and light. That she didn't ask for the whole thing on a silver platter—only that he love and adore her and the child that grew within her.

He didn't turn toward the capital or toward Redcliff. He turned the car around and drove back to the hospital.

CHAPTER SEVENTEEN

IT WOULD HAVE been impossible to hide the fact that she'd been crying when she finally left the hospital room, so Jenna didn't bother trying. Thankfully, after her dramatic entrance and re-sults, the nurses appeared comfortable assum-ing she was going to be fine.

Had it been worth it? Issuing an ultimatum to Sebastian like that—putting everything she wanted out there on the line. She thought so, even if inside she felt like a thousand tiny pieces of dull shattered glass scattered across asphalt.

Humpty Dumpty had a great fall. All the king's horses and all the king's... she thought idly, suddenly very clear on the fact that she needed some air, fresh air, not the recycled stuff circulating inside the hospital.

Outside the maternity ward now, strolling through the regular hospital, the word *king* bounced around in her head giddily.

She had ignored phone calls from the king. Multiple.

She stopped in her tracks, in the middle of the hallway between the chapel and an elevator bank. She needed to call Mina.

Changing course, she found the nearest courtesy phone and dialed quickly. And because she didn't just belong, she didn't just matter—rather, she shone wherever she went and made an irrefutable place for herself wherever she wanted—she was the kind of woman who had the queen's personal direct number memorized.

Mina picked up before the completion of the first ring.

"Hold on, I've got to get Hel on the line," she said, not giving Jenna a chance to protest.

Jenna smiled, the sound of her friend's voice and her rush to do things right as soothing to her soul as her mother's homemade chicken soup.

The call was short, her friends somehow sensing the delicate, easily tired nature of her new enlightenment, but it was more than enough. They would work out the details in the months to come, but she was returning to the queen's guard—and receiving all the associated maternity leave and pay.

She would need it now that she had drawn her line with Sebastian.

Stepping into the gray toned drizzle of the day was the final reset she needed.

She had come out a side entrance, one that

faced the rising rolls of hill that disappeared into fog that obscured the road to Redcliff.

Misty and green, quilted with distant farmsteads, much like her own family's, the view was one of her favorites in all of Cyrano—the view of home. Tourist brochures extolled the beaches and wine country, and locals adored the big city, but Jenna thought the sloping green landscape of the near interior leading all the way up to the upper reaches of the cliffs, was the most beautiful stretch of land of all.

Staring at it, her hair and dress and coat growing damp in the increasing rain, it wasn't enough that she could feel his memory in her body, she also saw Sebastian everywhere.

She saw him in the colors, in the harsh planes and valleys, in the red in the clay-rich soil. In the earliest days of Cyrano, Redcliff lands had extended all the way to the coast, including her family home. It was only after unification that Redcliff had become landlocked.

Perhaps that was why she had never worried about being out of place when she was with him—because they came from the same place, even if not the same walk of life.

Unlike with her closest friends, or within her career, or even back in the place she grew up, she had never felt out of place with Sebastian. The cosmic thing between them made everything ordinary and human that separated them—incredible wealth, titles, centuries-old traditions—seem small by comparison.

But even cosmic connection was not enough reason to settle.

They would either travel this road together as full partners or they wouldn't. It wasn't a path they could travel halfway and then turn around. That would be too hard on everyone's hearts.

Harder than the feeling in her heart now. At least now, she was the only one who had to deal with the pain of letting Sebastian go. If she had delayed, her child would have experienced this pain, too.

Turning her face up toward the rain, she let out a long sigh before setting out on her way home—not Sebastian's, which had somehow slipped into the mental definition, but the home she'd grown up in.

No one had answered the phone when she'd called her parents from the hospital room, but she lived only a few miles away. Even pregnant she could walk. Growing up in these hills, she'd walked in the rain many times before. It was too depressing to wait for a cab.

A little water was fine. It could hide her tears if she needed to have any more outbursts.

She was walking along the long hospital drive when the car pulled up beside her, slowing to drive at her walking speed.

It was Sebastian.

Jenna squinted through the rain and the tinted windows.

Her reflection staring back at her in the shiny glass assured her that her hair and dress were plastered to her, while her heart beat fast.

The streamlined contours of his car promised speed and intensity, the color that tempted you to look past it only to dare you to look away once you peeked. It blended in, even while it stood out. It kept secrets and watched with a thousand eyes. It was a spy, just like its creator.

It was a truly fantastic car, just like the man inside.

But she wasn't going to backtrack because he had a nice car.

She was thoroughly soaked to the bone and extremely sensitive to the fact that today pregnancy seemed to have stolen her soldier's toughness. Or perhaps that toughness had never been more than a thin facade. Maybe she was always a marshmallow.

She was a defender, there was no doubt of that, but maybe that was as far as it extended. Maybe she had never been hard, or smooth, or impenetrable, or whatever else it was people in the capital admired. And maybe it didn't matter. Maybe she could be a guard and still be soft, because that wasn't where her value and skill came from.

It had to be. Because that was who she was.

And she was both good enough and deserving.

The car doors hinged upward, and a dark figure stepped out.

"Jenna?" Sebastian asked.

"Sebastian." She lifted a hand to block the light from her eyes and watch the figure by the vehicle.

He stood there in the rainy, overcast afternoon, his clothes disheveled, face ravaged, but for the light that shone in his eyes. The same burning intensity that had changed her life that long-ago day on the balcony.

He opened his arms and she ran to him, sobbing once again as he picked her up, wrapped her in a hug so tight, she couldn't breathe and didn't care.

"I'm so sorry, Jenna. There's no excuse for leaving you like that, for what I said. I was a fool, and I'm sorry. I love you, Jenna. There is no other woman I would choose in the whole world to be the mother of my children, and no other woman I want, and therefore no other woman that I could possibly trust enough to spend the rest of my life with. Come back home with me. Be the mother of my child, yes, but more than that, be my wife."

He wasn't down on one knee. She didn't imagine he ever would be—at least not in public.

He was not the kind of man who knew how to bend. And he might be a little ruthless.

But he was hers, her home in the world, irrevocably and absolutely.

She spoke into his neck, clinging to him not for dear life, but for dear love. "Yes."

And then he was kissing her, long and hot and possessively, with so much passion she was surprised steam didn't rise from their soaked bodies.

He kissed away her fears that she was too plain, too poor and too Priory to ever find love.

He kissed away her fears that she would never truly belong in the capital, carving and viciously protecting an irrefutable and powerful place for herself by his side in the glittering world of wealth—a place in which she could be herself, raise her child and return to her job, a lifetime in the company of her two dearest friends becoming just the icing on the cake.

He kissed away her fears that he couldn't give them a real family, full of the kind of love that grew healthy, happy children, utterly obliterating every shadow of a doubt that haunted or lingered.

Sebastian loved her but didn't *only* love her.

It went far deeper than that.

They kissed, standing in the pouring rain until she wasn't sure where she ended and he began, and then he led her to the car that she wasn't sure wasn't a spaceship and drove them back home, to Redcliff.

There, they would make a home for their family—honest, wholehearted, and utterly unique. And for the times when work meant they would need to stay in the capital for a longer stretch of time, they could create a new private paradise, designed by Sebastian and brought to life by the energy that flared to life when two pieces that fit together found their perfect, destined whole.

EPILOGUE

Two years later

"I'M GLAD WE'RE in agreement, gentlemen." Sebastian raised the toast, and the two men he spoke to touched their glasses to one another's.

Sebastian, Zayn and Drake were arranged in a half circle—Sebastian standing, Drake and Zayn seated—set apart at the outdoor bar from the soft grassy play area where three women formed a small ring around a trio of tiny seated humans, the babbles and ham-fisted gestures of which seemed to indicate the beginnings of a beautiful friendship.

Each of the tiny humans hovered around ten months old. The two girls, the Royal Princess Elke Aldenia d'Argonia and the young Amira Andros, heiress to the largest duchy in Cyrano, were both sturdier in their seat than the lone boy, but Reynard made up for the fact that he kept collapsing with the volume and power of his voice at each tumble.

Sebastian's son was a talker. More of a roarer, actually.

So much so that, while it remained as strong as ever, an enduring flame, the peace Sebastian found at his many homes was no longer a quiet peace.

It was, however, still rooted in Jenna. Always Jenna.

It blew him away to reflect on the era of transformation that she had ushered into his life. There had been more fraught and tenuous firsts than a man as jaded as himself had a right to.

He cherished every one, bringing to family life the same focused intensity he brought to everything on the short list of things he loved, a list that included: Jenna, his child, espionage and architecture. It wasn't lost on him that her coming into his life had nearly doubled the list. She'd gone and grown his heart to nearly twice its original size.

And it was twice as much to love her with.

He loved her with the immensity of his full will behind him.

He'd gained much to lose, but if he was more vulnerable now than he had ever been, it was because he loved more, and was therefore justified in being that much more cunning and ruthless in removing any threat thereto.

And this was a part of the reason the three

men held their small conference at the sunny poolside bar.

Each man held a drink: the king, the pirate and the spy.

It was a good setup for a punch line.

It was an even better setup for an ironclad national protection team.

By land, by sea, by shadow—they would watch and guide Cyrano into its bright, modern future—as directed by their wives, of course. Their children needed a playground, after all.

The three men had just finished their toast, officially setting Sebastian's latest plan in motion.

The king was Zayn d'Argonia. His role needed no explanation. His job was to rule. He was the king.

The pirate was Duke Drake Andros, now the wealthiest landholder in the nation. He was also a retired admiral and privateer who had reclaimed his birthright and in the process found the love of his life in Helene d'Tierrza.

He would watch the seas—a critical role for an island nation.

And then there was Sebastian, the reformed playboy duke, now a world-renowned architect. Publicly, he had become the incredibly exclusive architect who designed only three houses a year. Privately, his hands were filled with adoring his small family and leading Cyrano's intelligence forces.

Three men, tied to one another through the country they ran and the women that ran them.

They were colleagues and, after the past year and a half or so, friends—a rare thing for men as powerful as they were.

And it was all because of the eagle-eyed women who stood at a distance from them, watching over their babies.

His Jenna, Queen Mina and the Duchess Andros—or, more truly, the queen and her loyal guards and most trusted companions, as story-book worthy as the Three Musketeers.

But for Sebastian, there was only Jenna.

After taking his fiancée home that day in the rain, they had flowed right into a honeymoon-like bubble, exploring the rest of Redcliff and each other simultaneously.

He lured her the same way every time, and she always indulged him.

"Let me show you the greenhouse," he would say.

And she would go.

"Let me show you the pools."

And she would go.

And so on and so on, until she was glowing and he was inspired to build more houses.

He began drawing up plans for their home in the capital immediately after they returned home that day.

Not too long later, and after many sumptuous dinners, Jenna was into her wonderfully energized and nausea-free third trimester and the specs for their townhome were complete. They had enjoyed their private library many, many times. Now they were ready to return to the city.

And, possibly because of all the home-cooked food, to his, her, and her entire family's delight, the bump they'd been waiting for and despairing of ever seeing finally made an appearance.

The king and queen celebrated their wedding in December, the date moved up to accommodate the queen's pregnancy, and it was such a stunning winter ceremony it set off a new cold-weather wedding trend.

The queen shocked the world and none who knew her by choosing her two guards as her bridesmaids. And then, one by one, the babies had arrived. Mina's, then Helene's, and then Jenna's.

Helene had delivered early and Jenna late, after all the plans had been made and executed.

All the babies were happy and healthy and wealthy.

His son was the cutest—in Sebastian's well-informed opinion.

Following in the footsteps of his father instead of his mother, Little Reynard had not arrived in the early morning but waited until the night was at its darkest point to make his debut.

Before his son's birth, Sebastian had known Jenna was strong—a woman with a warrior spirit.

After, he feared her for the goddess that she was.

He might have the power to pull strings and make nations move, but she pulled life from the unknown and brought it screaming, whole and healthy into the world.

And of course, just two weeks before Reynard's arrival, he and Jenna had been married, the occasion taking place on a sunny spring day at Redcliff.

At Sebastian's insistence, the ceremony had been outrageously expensive. To Jenna's delight, it was suffused with earthy warmth and love.

Jenna's mother had made her dress. Helene and Queen Mina and her sisters-in-law were bridesmaids.

With colorful silk ribbons and flowers, an abundance of handmade lace, and iced lemon and ginger chiffon cake—imported from faraway producers and hothouses or handmade—surrounded by the people she loved most in the world, the wedding had been everything Jenna had ever wanted. She'd made a point of both telling and showing him afterward.

He had appreciated the sentiment, but Sebastian needed no thanks. Jenna coming down the aisle in her layers of lace and satin, the empire waist and deep-V cut of her dress setting off the warm glow of her olive skin and glorious fullness of her breasts, her long hair loose and flowing beneath the veil that rested atop her head like a medieval lady's—also handcrafted by her mother—all for him was all he would ever need.

She had been so beautiful that, after the queen got permission to share a photo on her social media channels, a bridal magazine asked to purchase photos from their day for a special edition.

Jenna's embarrassed shock at the request would always make Sebastian smile. She had no idea that becoming a trendsetter came along with becoming the Duchess of Redcliff.

She would get used to it as time went on, but he doubted she would ever feel invisible again.

He didn't worry that the attention would change her. She would always remain his honest and true Jenna, no matter how many people took notice, just as he would always be wicked and she would always love him anyway.

The fact of it never failed to give him pause.

She saw him, complicated and shadowed, and loved him anyway, shared her light, let him drink his fill over and over, never minding the endless ravenous hunger he had for it. Jenna had made him do a double take, and so he had taken her. And he would, again and again, until the two of them were no more, and all the world was left to their children.

A world he intended to preserve and protect from every threat—political, economic and environmental—so that those children might enjoy it half as well as Jenna had taught him to. That would be enough.

And because of the miracle that she was, he wasn't alone in the endeavor.

He had her, and he had the men at his side.

"Now, stop that, Amira," Helene shouted suddenly. "You leave Auntie Jenna's braid alone!"

Swirling the ice around in his drink, listening to the satisfying clink of the frigid cubes against the priceless crystal, and the happy chaos around him, Sebastian took a sip.

The cool liquid burned down his throat, its fire nowhere near a match for the one that burned in his eyes as he observed the woman with a long dark braid and the green-eyed little boy who sat at her feet, his dark mop a match for her own—Jenna and Reynard—his whole world.

They had faced their dragons, hunted down and worked out the scars from the past that hindered them, and because of it, Sebastian realized, even more important than their impressive lineages and legacies, their children would not inherit their wounds. And what was that, if not happily-ever-after?

* * * * *

If you couldn't put
Pregnant After One Forbidden Night *down,*
why not catch the first and second instalments
in The Queen's Guard trilogy,
Stolen to Wear His Crown
and His Stolen Innocent's Vow.

And don't forget to look out for more
stories by Marcella Bell!